MURDER ON THE BOARDWALK

A ROSA REED MYSTERY

LEE STRAUSS
DENISE JADEN

Cover by Steven Novak

Illustrations by Amanda Sorensen

Library and Archives Canada Cataloguing in Publication Title: Murder on the Boardwalk : a 1950s cozy historical mystery / Lee Strauss. Names: Strauss, Lee (Novelist), author. Description: Series statement: A Rosa Reed mystery ; 2 Identifiers: Canadiana (print) 20200181343 | Canadiana (ebook) 20200181351 | ISBN 9781774090916 (hardcover) | ISBN 9781774090923 (softcover) | ISBN 9781774090930 (IngramSpark softcover) | ISBN 9781774090893 (EPUB) | ISBN 9781774090909 (Kindle) Classification: LCC PS8637.T739 M98 2020 | DDC C813/.6—dc23

MORE FROM LEE STRAUSS

On AMAZON

THE ROSA REED MYSTERIES

(1950s cozy historical)

Murder at High Tide

Murder on the Boardwalk

Murder at the Bomb Shelter

Murder on Location

Murder and Rock 'n Roll

GINGER GOLD MYSTERY SERIES (cozy 1920s historical)

Cozy. Charming. Filled with Bright Young Things. This Jazz Age murder mystery will entertain and delight you with its 1920s flair and pizzazz!

Murder on the SS Rosa

Murder at Hartigan House

Murder at Bray Manor

Murder at Feathers & Flair

Murder at the Mortuary

Murder at Kensington Gardens

Murder at St. George's Church

The Wedding of Ginger & Basil

Murder Aboard the Flying Scotsman

Murder at the Boat Club

Murder on Eaton Square

Murder by Plum Pudding

Murder on Fleet Street

LADY GOLD INVESTIGATES (Ginger Gold companion short stories)

Volume 1

Volume 2

Volume 3

HIGGINS & HAWKE MYSTERY SERIES (cozy 1930s historical)

The 1930s meets Rizzoli & Isles in this friendship depression era cozy mystery series.

Death at the Tavern

Death on the Tower

Death on Hanover

A NURSERY RHYME MYSTERY SERIES(mystery/sci fi)

Marlow finds himself teamed up with intelligent and savvy Sage Farrell, a girl so far out of his league he feels blinded in her presence - literally - damned glasses! Together they work to find the identity of @gingerbreadman. Can they stop the killer before he strikes again?

Gingerbread Man

Life Is but a Dream

Hickory Dickory Dock

Twinkle Little Star

THE PERCEPTION TRILOGY (YA dystopian mystery)

Zoe Vanderveen is a GAP—a genetically altered person. She lives in the security of a walled city on prime water-front property alongside other equally beautiful people with extended life spans. Her brother Liam is missing. Noah Brody, a boy on the outside, is the only one who can help ~ but can she trust him?

Perception

Volition

Contrition

LIGHT & LOVE (sweet romance)

Set in the dazzling charm of Europe, follow Katja, Gabriella,

Eva, Anna and Belle as they find strength, hope and love.

Sing me a Love Song

Your Love is Sweet

In Light of Us

Lying in Starlight

PLAYING WITH MATCHES (WW2 history/romance)

A sobering but hopeful journey about how one young German boy copes with the war and propaganda. Based on true events.

A Piece of Blue String (companion short story)

THE CLOCKWISE COLLECTION (YA time travel romance)

Casey Donovan has issues: hair, height and uncontrollable trips to the 19th century! And now this ~ she's accidentally taken Nate Mackenzie, the cutest boy in the school, back in time. Awkward.

Clockwise

Clockwiser

Like Clockwork

Counter Clockwise

Clockwork Crazy

Clocked (companion novella)

Standalones

Seaweed

Love, Tink

1

Lines of gently swaying palm trees and stucco Spanish mansions were set against a cloudless blue sky, and Miss Rosa Reed, known in rainy London, England as WPC Reed of the Metropolitan Police, thought the endless sunshine would never get old. She strolled away from the Forrester mansion in Santa Bonita, California, with her cousin Gloria at her side.

"We need to find you a fuller crinoline," Gloria said, playfully nudging Rosa with an elbow as they neared one of the Forrester vehicles, a two-tone yellow Chevrolet Bel Air parked in the driveway.

Not once in her life in London had Rosa been criticized for her wardrobe. With a mother who owned one of London's highbrow Regent Street dress shops, Rosa had grown up under the influence of stylish and quality fashion, the kind that certainly turned heads in the United Kingdom. Apparently, the California coast was a different story as Rosa had been encouraged more than once to wear something a little brighter, a little tighter, or today, a little fuller.

Then again, those suggestions had come from Gloria and might have said more about Rosa's spirited cousin than they did about California fashions. Already, Rosa regretted giving in to Gloria's pleas to accompany her to the fair recently set up at the boardwalk. Rosa preferred the quiet of her bedroom —hers at the Forrester mansion felt as cozy and comfortable as her room at Hartigan House in South Kensington—and a good book. Rosa had a stack resting on her night table, from mystery fiction to the latest in forensic science developments. She'd raided the Forrester mansion library shortly after she'd arrived in Santa Bonita, and had tipped one of the maids to make a run to the local library for her (not daring to go there herself for reasons she'd rather not think of at this time). The gentle purring and warm companionship of her kitten, Diego, was all the socializing Rosa desired, and with a deep breath she had to brace herself for the cacophony sure to come.

Not wanting to face Gloria's wrath if she changed her mind, Rosa was determined to be a good sport. Gloria looked adorable and rather youthful—seven years Rosa's junior, Rosa often felt ancient at twenty-eight in Gloria's presence—in her pink flared skirt with an embroidery of a sizable French poodle and flat black-and-white leather saddleback shoes.

Gloria stood with one hand on one tiny hip and the other stretched out, palm open. "Keys?"

"Why?"

"You've driven it *all* week. Besides, you have Diego to concern yourself with."

Rosa peeked into her tapestry handbag, or *satchel*, as she liked to call it, where her kitten slept soundly. She'd chosen the satchel more for the comfort of Diego, a brown tabby kitten Rosa had recently rescued, than she had for how it complimented her sky-blue swing dress—the one without a large enough crinoline, apparently—and matching Juliette cap.

Diego had an adventurous personality and didn't, for the most part, cause Rosa any concern when she took him along. A rather fortuitous discovery, since Aunt Louisa had insisted that Rosa keep the kitten with her and not leave "that scraggly thing" behind unless either Gloria or the Forrester housekeeper, Señora Gomez, was available to watch him.

Rosa suppressed her strong feelings of apprehension as she handed over the coveted keys. "Drive carefully!" With an exaggerated shudder, she added, "The way you command a car reminds me of my mum."

"Oh, I love Aunt Ginger!" Gloria smirked at Rosa before snatching the keys. "I don't suppose you'd like to trade mothers?" She laughed before Rosa could come up with a suitable quip and hopped into the driver's side of the Bel Air. In moments, the large engine rumbled to life.

"Why Do Fools Fall in Love" played on the radio, and Rosa mused at how apropos it was for her, the fool who fell in love with Miguel Belmonte, her former American flame and who, as fate would have it, was no longer single.

Gloria, looking away from the road more often than Rosa would have liked, announced, "I'm sure we'll see people I know at the boardwalk. In fact, you might run into some of your friends from high school."

Though born and raised in London, Rosa had spent her high school years in Santa Bonita. Her parents had felt an urgent need to get her out of harm's way during the Second World War, and Rosa suspected some of that angst was due to their involvement with the British secret service, though she could never get them to admit to it to her.

The highway wound along the coast. As Gloria chattered on about the funfair at the boardwalk, Rosa gazed at the gleaming sun. The ball of fire hung over the beach, and blue water rushed to the shore. The scene looked like a postcard picture. In the distance, she saw the Santa Bonita Pier. Bright red bars lined a giant Ferris wheel at the edge of the water.

Almost missing the exit, Gloria stomped on the brake and spun onto the ramp to guide them off the highway just in time.

"Gloria!" Rosa pressed a hand on the Bel Air's sleek crocus-yellow dashboard. "For crying out loud!"

"Oh, chili-pop, honey." Gloria glided around a bend that momentarily hid the ocean, then continued along a curvy road that led them down a steep decline. Rosa didn't relax until they were level with the water.

Gloria managed to squeeze into a parking spot without scratching the paint. Rosa could only imagine how Clarence, Gloria's older brother, took to the odd scuffs sure to appear on the Forrester vehicles.

Rosa reached for her satchel. Diego was awake and no worse for wear.

"Hi, sweetie," Rosa cooed and reached in to pat him. "You've already had your first fair ride, poor thing."

Gloria pretended offense, blowing loudly through lips thick with tangerine-colored lipstick. She led the way to the back of the gravel parking lot and down a short dirt path. Then, quite suddenly, the trail opened to more bright colors and tiny lights than Rosa had ever seen in one place. It was as though Christmas had come early and had exploded across the pier.

"It's stunning!" Rosa said, stopping. Now that they were closer, she could see not only the brightly lit Ferris wheel set against the brilliant blue sky, but also several carnival game tents, a ride with spinning cars, and even a roller coaster! The salty air she'd become accustomed to in the last two weeks took on a new aroma with smells of buttered popcorn and warm sugar.

"It is, isn't it?" Gloria grasped Rosa's hand and pulled her toward the lights and the action.

"You'll have to show me how it's all done," Rosa said while gazing around in awe. She slid her new Riviera sunglasses up onto her forehead to get a clearer view.

They walked onto the base of the pier, and only then could Rosa see most of the exciting ocean-side fair. A large platform sat inland and seemed to hold most of the amusement rides, including the giant roller coaster that made Rosa's stomach turn upside down just watching it. The Ferris wheel turned its slow and steady circles at the farthest end of the pier. Along the boardwalk and pier, numerous game tents were busy with customers and "carnies" yelling, "Step right up! Be our next winner!"

As Rosa and Gloria meandered down the pier, the dings and clanks and shouts from the carnival games were soon drowned out by lively upbeat swing music.

"Is there a band here?" Rosa asked.

Gloria answered glibly, "Mick and the Beat Boys are playing tonight. They're often here on weekends. Isn't that neat?"

Rosa's pulse jumped at the mention of the band's name. The "Mick" in question was the nickname of Detective Miguel Belmonte. She groaned inwardly. So much for keeping her distance from the man.

Very few people knew of the short but intense romance she and Miguel Belmonte had shared eleven years ago. *Eleven years.* The four months they'd spent falling in love was just a blip now on Rosa's timeline. Ancient history. But despite her best efforts, her body still reacted to the mention of his name.

"There's an amphitheater just ahead, with a dance floor." As Gloria led the way, a gaggle of ladies that Gloria recognized joined them. She called out hello and waved, and the gaggle moved toward them. Turning to Rosa, she added, "See, I told you we'd know people here."

We seemed like the wrong pronoun, but as Gloria leaned for quick hugs, recognition dawned. A few *were* familiar to Rosa, and one was *particularly* familiar.

A lack of teachers during Rosa's high school years in Santa Bonita had combined students of all ages in large classrooms. More times than Rosa could count, they had turned out the school lights and blacked out windows when an oil field was bombed, or a firebomb was discovered somewhere within California.

"You remember Marjorie, right?" Gloria said, motioning to a pretty girl in a green A-line dress with a black-and-white polka-dotted under layer. She wore her bright-red hair in a long ponytail.

"Rosa Reed!" Marjorie said with a sparkle in her eye. "It's so nice to see you." She sprang forward to give Rosa a hug, which momentarily surprised Rosa. This very non-English custom of hugging at every hello and goodbye took some getting used to.

"Hello!" Rosa said. Marjorie Davidson had transformed from a girl to a woman in the eleven years Rosa had been gone. "You're all grown up!"

Rosa recognized Joyce Kilbourne and Pauline Van Peridon before Gloria could announce them.

"Hello, ladies," Rosa said. They both wore less flashy dresses, Joyce, a slender brunette in violet and Pauline with a boyish-figure, in navy. If anyone needed a fuller crinoline, it was Pauline.

"Hi, Rosa."

Pauline's voice was soft and gentle. Rosa remembered how Pauline had suffered from shyness as a child.

"Hi, Pauline. So nice to see you again."

Pauline covered her mouth when she said, "I forgot all about your accent!"

"I'd argue that you're the ones with the accent," Rosa said warmly.

Joyce grasped both of Rosa's hands, leaned in, and kissed her on the cheek. "Oh, Rosa! It's been too long."

To the brunette who had only just stepped into the group behind Marjorie, Gloria said, "And you must remember Nancy."

Rosa's emotions were in a state of disorder as she stared at the young lady with honey-blond hair who gaped back. Older now, Nancy Davidson—now Kline—had her hair styled shorter, and a little more weight rested on her hips and face, but her round blue eyes and cute ski-jump nose were unmistakable.

"Hello, Nancy," Rosa said, stepping closer.

Nancy had been Rosa's American best friend during her days in Santa Bonita through the war years. Practically attached at the hip, they'd done homework together, discovered fashion and boys together, and ultimately, Nancy was the only one to know about Rosa's forbidden affair with Miguel Belmonte.

The girls had continued to write after Rosa returned to London, but like with Miguel, the effort became too difficult over time. Because Nancy had invited Rosa to her wedding, Rosa had felt compelled to ask Nancy to hers. She had not expected Nancy would come. Or reply, for that matter, and she hadn't.

Without smiling, Nancy said, "I heard you were back in town."

Whether Gloria's impulse to pull the other girls away was an act of sensitivity or merely a need to move things along, Rosa was thankful for a moment to speak with Nancy alone.

"I've been meaning to look you up."

"Uh-huh."

"I ran into your mother the other day at the bakery. She said you've been busy. Three boys?"

"Yes, Eddie junior, Johnny, and Mikey, ages ten, eight, and six." Nancy risked a smile. "A right handful. Mom's a champ about taking them occasionally so I can forget I'm an old married woman and pretend to be Marjorie's age again."

Rosa returned the smile. "It's why I like hanging out with Gloria."

"Are you here on your honeymoon?" Nancy's eyes darted about in search of Rosa's phantom spouse.

Rosa frowned. "I didn't go through with the wedding." Rosa had done a horrible thing to Lord Winston Eveleigh and walked, rather *run*, out of St. George's Church before saying *I do*. "It's a good thing you didn't come."

Nancy's eyes brightened, and Rosa saw a glimpse of her old friend in them. "Golly! Now that sounds like a story I'd like to hear!"

2

Diego poked his fuzzy little face through the opening of Rosa's satchel and meowed.

Nancy jumped. "Holy moly!"

Rosa bit back her grin. "This is Diego. I found him behind the bakery just before I ran into your mother."

Nancy let out a sharp laugh. "I wondered why you were carrying such an ugly bag. I thought all your fashion sense had gone by the wayside or something."

"It's purely practical." Rosa lifted Diego out of the satchel and kissed his head, silently thanking him for breaking the ice.

"Oh, he's so sweet," Nancy cooed. "Can I hold him?"

"Of course."

As Nancy snuggled Diego, her eyes went shiny with sympathy. "I'm sorry it didn't work out with your lord."

Rosa had to laugh at that. "All those titles and class differences sound very posh from this side of the world."

Nancy limply flapped her palm. "Very *posh*. You sound so English, Rosa."

"Well, I am rather English."

"I suppose." Nancy eyed Rosa as she handed back Diego. "You know who's playing in the band?"

"Yes," Rosa said without catching Nancy's gaze. "Gloria mentioned it."

"Eddie's over there already, with some of his buddies. I'm headed that way."

Rosa glanced about for Gloria and saw she and her friends were halfway there too.

"I'm fine," Rosa said. "Miguel and I have already become reacquainted, and he has a fiancée now. I'm fine."

Nancy narrowed her eyes knowingly. "You've said that twice."

"Then it must be true."

Rosa thought she could easily hang out with Gloria and Nancy and the others and not watch the band. She had Diego to keep her distracted. Right? However, when she rounded the corner to the amphitheater, the first person she saw was Miguel, front and center, on the stage—a guitar slung across a shoulder.

His black hair was oiled back and, for the occasion, styled with a duckbill fringe which hovered over a brow shiny with moisture from the afternoon heat. He and his band members wore casual clothes for this beachside show—khaki-colored pants and short-sleeve, button-down shirts—but all Rosa could see were Miguel's dimples and copper-brown eyes.

"Are you coming?" Gloria asked, skipping back toward Rosa to grab her hand. Rosa had unintentionally stopped in place. Nodding numbly, she moved forward with her cousin as she tore her eyes from the stage.

Rosa hadn't seen so many poodle skirts in one place before, and the fascination with saddle shoes became apparent as she watched the guys spin the girls around. They were perfect for sliding across the waxed floor.

The color and music intoxicated Rosa, and she took a moment to recognize Nancy, already out on the dance floor with an older version of Eddie Kline. Nancy's blue swing skirt spun out around her with each of her twists and turns. Marjorie had also partnered up.

Rosa and Gloria didn't have to wait long on the fringes before being approached by two good-looking fellows dressed in plain plaid button-downs and cotton slacks which were cuffed at the ankles and showed glimpses of pairs of colorful dress socks. One of them spoke for them both. "Would you ladies like to dance?"

Rosa held up her satchel. "I'm sorry, but I have my kitten with me." She turned to Gloria, trying to assess her cousin's eagerness to dance. The way her feet were tapping, Rosa thought she could safely assume she was ready to twirl. "You go ahead."

Gloria linked arms with one of the men and the other took his leave. Rosa felt bad that he hadn't bothered to ask either Joyce or Pauline to dance. Only a second later, Joyce proclaimed, "I'm going for some lemonade," and headed for a nearby stand. Rosa hoped Joyce hadn't sensed her pity.

Mick and the Beat Boys rang the first note of "That'll Be the Day", and many of the dance partners changed. Gloria disappeared into the fray, and Marjorie spun into the middle with a new partner, a shorter man in a trim short-sleeved cotton shirt, summer slacks, and a pair of leather shoes.

Music was Rosa's enemy! All the lyrics of the most popular songs seemed to apply to some point and time in Rosa and Miguel's short but emotional romance. *You say you're going to leave, you know it's a lie, cuz that'll be the day when I die.*

Rosa had left, but Miguel hadn't died.

"That's my brother, Henry," Pauline said, pulling Rosa out of her reverie.

Rosa blinked and focused on the movement on the dance floor. "Which one?"

"He's dancing the jive with Marjorie."

Rosa admired the quick-footed work performed by each partner as they held hands loosely, breaking apart and coming together again on the beat.

Clearly, they'd danced together before. "Oh, are they sweethearts?"

"No, no," Pauline said quickly. "He's too old for her."

Rosa hummed, thinking that she'd heard that one before, but said nothing.

Pauline wistfully added, "The jive is my favorite dance, I think. It looks like such fun."

Rosa agreed. "Especially if you have the right dance partner."

Inexplicably, Rosa's gaze shot back to Miguel. She pinched her eyes and shook her head as if that would help rid it of unwanted thoughts. Unbidden, her mind went to a time when she and Miguel had danced hand in hand to Vera Lynn singing the 1943 hit "We'll Meet Again". The rich sounds of brass instruments in the orchestra added to the emotions behind Vera Lynn's husky voice, "*Don't know where, don't know when...*"

Finally, and blessedly, the music stopped. Rosa's friends separated from their dance partners and made their way over, bringing Rosa a welcome distraction.

Nancy motioned to her husband. "You remember Eddie."

Rosa smiled. "Of course. Nice to see you again."

"You haven't changed a bit," Eddie said, arms wide and beckoning. "Give us a hug."

Rosa held in her dismay and leaned in to Eddie sideways, keeping her shoulder to his chest. Eddie wore round glasses and was thicker around the middle than she remembered, but his gray shorts and baby-blue button-down matched Nancy beautifully, and they looked good together.

Marjorie spoke in a loud whisper that commanded the ladies' attention. "Ooh, did any of you see who's working on the boardwalk now?" She punctuated two names that Rosa recognized. "Victor. Boyd."

Victor Boyd, more than anyone Rosa had gone to school with, had been a memorable character. When she had first arrived in Santa Bonita in 1941, she'd had a difficult time making friends. Many of the other kids thought her accent was strange, and the war had made everyone, even children and youths, suspicious of anyone different. She'd been an immediate outcast.

An outcast himself, Victor Boyd had come to Rosa's defense. Rosa would never forget how he had stood up to the other students and told them to stop mocking her accent. He didn't seem to care when the bullying turned to him instead.

"Remember when we were supposed to be on blackout, and he started to flash the lights in the classroom?" Joyce said.

"Oh, and the way he used to sabotage my parts count at the aircraft plant," Nancy added. "I'd end up assembling only half of the daily quota and getting in trouble for it?"

During the war, the older girls had all worked together after school at the local aircraft plant. Nancy had been the most adept by far at assembling parts and rewiring components.

Giddy laughs erupted among them as they shared stories. Rosa thought it odd to hear the lighthearted lilts to their voices. In reality, it had been such a bleak time.

After taking a long gulp of her lemonade, Joyce added, "But Pauline had it the worst."

"He teased you about being a tomboy, huh, Pauline?" Nancy said.

Rosa recalled how Pauline had come to classes in overalls and baseball caps, while the rest of her female classmates wore dresses, stockings, and matching Mary Janes. Pauline's mother had passed away around that time, and her father—a well-respected mechanic and weapons expert—didn't quite know how to take care of his only daughter. He died tragically as well, and his death had made headline news in Santa Bonita.

Pauline's lip twitched, but she didn't respond to Nancy's comment. She kept her gaze glued to her hands, clasped at her waist.

Joyce missed seeing Pauline's discomfort and continued, "He was always making jokes about offering you up for the draft."

"Victor picked on me," Gloria added sourly, "and I was just a little kid. He should pay for all the awful things he did."

Marjorie motioned for the group to follow her.

"Come on. Let's go see. I wonder if he's gotten fat and bald!"

A snicker emanated from the ladies as they jumped to follow Marjorie. Rosa checked on Diego, awake but playing with his cloth mouse, then feeling morbidly curious, followed the girls.

Away from the music of the band, clanging bells and hooting whistles filled the air. Chatter and screams drifted from happy riders.

Rosa stood in awe by the giant roller coaster and its yellow and blue sign that read, "The Sea Viper". Her breath caught in her throat as the loud *clack, clack, clack* of the cars on the track reverberated through her whole body. She had always felt better when she was in control of a vehicle. Letting Gloria or her mother drive felt risky enough for her. The track wound around in snake-like fashion, and for a long moment, Rosa couldn't pull her gaze away.

"There! Look!" Marjorie said in an excited whisper. "There's Victor Boyd!"

Wearing a black T-shirt, stretched over what was now a paunch of a belly, and grubby jeans, Rosa immediately recognized the former bully. He still had most of his hair, though it looked like it hadn't been trimmed in six months. As a carnie ride operator, he hadn't exactly reached the height of an accomplished life.

Rosa wasn't alone in thinking this. Nancy harrumphed and said, "Well, there you go. At least fate gave him what was coming."

"Are you kidding me?" Marjorie asked, not trying to be quiet in the least. There was a good chance Victor could hear her. "After everything he did to you girls? He doesn't deserve a job in our beautiful town."

Joyce chimed in. "I agree!"

Gloria, still a few feet back, looked as though she was surveying the rest of the fair, and Rosa sensed she'd lost interest in Victor Boyd.

However, at the loud voices of their friends, Victor turned his head and stared straight at them. His attention was unnerving, and everyone stopped talking at once—like a drove of baaing sheep suddenly aware of a wolf in their midst.

His dark-eyed gaze locked onto Rosa and she couldn't stop herself from offering a small wave. He didn't wave back.

"Enough about *him,*" Nancy finally said. She flapped a hand at the roller coaster. "Let's get back to dancing!"

3

Some of Rosa's fondest childhood memories were of her parents dancing. Basil and Ginger Reed were renowned for their fancy footwork on the dance floor, whether it was the waltz, a Latin tango, or old-time Charleston. So, it wasn't surprising that Rosa had a fondness for music and dancing herself. Watching these young people back at the bandstand dancing the boogie-woogie and the jitterbug had Rosa's feet tapping and her heart smiling.

Nancy, Marjorie, Joyce, and Gloria had all once again taken quickly to the dance floor with partners. Though Rosa would've loved to dance, she wasn't prepared to do so with a stranger, especially so soon after breaking off an engagement. But even if she had been ready to dance with someone new, there was no way on God's green earth she would stumble about under the spotlights with Miguel on stage and watching.

Diego earned his weight in gold, as time after time she produced him as an excuse to say no to a disappointed young man, most of whom found patting her kitten's soft head strangely reconciliatory.

Miguel moved around the stage fluidly and looked more like the youthful and spirited soldier Rosa knew in the mid-forties than the police detective with whom she had recently become reacquainted. Despite her best efforts, Rosa couldn't stop watching him on stage.

And Miguel watched her too.

Rosa quickly averted her eyes. How embarrassing to be caught staring!

What she and Miguel had once shared was lost with the past, and so much had happened since then, even more than her near marriage to Winston.

Rosa shook her head. She didn't want to think about Lord Winston Eveleigh—to think of her former fiancé was to think about his sister. Vivien Eveleigh had been Rosa's closest friend in London, and her murder, still unsolved, had shattered Rosa's heart.

Pauline was the only one of the former school friends who, like Rosa, stayed off the dance floor, though in Pauline's case, sadly, it was because no one had asked her. If only ladies could dance together, Rosa herself would have asked Pauline to dance.

"Are you having fun?" Rosa asked, attempting to draw the shy girl out.

"Oh, sure," Pauline said, then looked away as if frightened Rosa might ask her another question.

Impulsively, Rosa held out her kitten. "This is Diego."

On cue, Diego let out a sweet little "mew" to greet Pauline. Diego didn't seem to react to the loud music and carnival noises. Her kitten seemed up for anything.

Pauline reached over to scratch Diego under the chin, and he held his head back as if asking for more.

"Would you like to hold him?" Rosa asked.

Pauline's eyes warmed, and Rosa had the feeling the girl preferred her friends to have fur on them. After placing Diego into Pauline's hands, Rosa continued to scratch the soft hair around his neck.

"Aren't you a sweety-pie," Pauline cooed as though the kitten was the one needing reassurance.

Rosa could picture Pauline at home with several cats. Perhaps that was where she did most of her talking.

In silent agreement, Rosa and Pauline sat on a nearby bench as the band broke into another song, and the dancers did the *cha-cha*. This dance was a favorite of Rosa's, and her toes tapped along. Diego, not nearly as caught up in the band or the music, kneaded his tiny paws on Pauline's lap.

Nancy danced with Eddie, who Rosa uncharitably thought had two left feet. Despite their clumsy turn about the dance floor, they were both laughing and looked to be having fun. Marjorie danced with a sturdy-looking guy with blond hair and a skinny mustache, so it appeared that Henry Van Peridon wasn't her only choice. Joyce and a very tall man with a bowling-style shirt left the floor to get drinks from the vendor on the other side of the room. The way he gazed with affection at Joyce made Rosa think this wasn't their first dance together.

Gloria and her dance partner, a handsome Asian man, drew a round of applause from onlookers. Rosa was astounded by how good they were. Dance genes obviously ran in the family.

When the song ended, Gloria strutted toward Rosa and Pauline, out of breath and glistening.

"Who were you dancing with?" Rosa asked.

"Oh, just a fellow in need of a partner."

"You're both terrific."

"Ah, thanks, Rosa. Now, if you'll excuse me, I'm going to find a restroom."

"I saw some on our way in." Rosa pointed to the portable lavatory stalls they'd passed near the carnival tents, but Gloria wrinkled her nose.

"I'll just walk down to the Surfside Lobster Bar. Mom knows the manager. They'll let me use their facilities." She pointed beyond the pier and down to a seaside restaurant, which was lit by a neon sign.

Neon lighting was another big change in the town since Rosa had last been in California. As far as the eye could see, bright pink, orange, and yellow lights dotted different beachfront establishments all down the shoreline. It was especially spectacular after dark.

"It looks like quite a walk," Rosa said. "Would you like me to come with you?" She glanced at her purring kitten.

Gloria was already moving away from the bench and waved a casual hand. "I'll be back in a jiffy. They probably don't want too many non-eating patrons barging in anyway."

Moments later, still laughing and breathing hard from dancing, Marjorie and Nancy made their way to Rosa. She didn't notice where their dance partners had disappeared to, but Joyce and the tall man continued to spin around the dance floor together.

"Come on! We're going on the *wonder wheel*," Marjorie said.

Rosa didn't know what a "wonder wheel" was, but Pauline stood, lifting Diego off her lap. Rosa accepted the kitten into her arms. "I should stay until Gloria gets back," she said. It wouldn't do for them to get parted in this crowd.

"I caught her on her way out," Marjorie said. "She's going to meet us at the ride platform later."

"And what about Joyce?"

"She and her husband, Don, said they're leaving after this dance."

Joyce had a husband? That was why she hadn't felt embarrassed at not being asked to dance earlier. "Is he that tall fellow?"

Marjorie chuckled. "Don Welks is nearly seven feet tall! Joyce looks like a child next to him."

Rosa tucked Diego back into her satchel and followed them. It wasn't until Marjorie tugged her toward the end of the dock, not the rides, that she understood.

"Oh! The Ferris wheel?" As she hurried to keep up, Rosa took another peek into her handbag. Even through all the commotion, or perhaps because of it, Diego had fallen asleep again. She hadn't thought she'd be braving any rides tonight with Diego with her, but she'd always wanted to ride a Ferris wheel, and from the looks of things, her kitten would sleep right through it.

With the band and dance going strong, there was almost no lineup for the Ferris wheel.

"Where did Eddie go?" Rosa asked Nancy after noticing he was missing.

"He went home. He has an early shift tomorrow." Nancy went on ahead and paired up with Pauline on the platform for the next Ferris wheel car. For a moment, Rosa felt a little hurt that Nancy hadn't linked arms with her, but time had changed many things, and her friendship with Nancy was one of them.

Marjorie pulled Rosa onto the Ferris wheel with her. The rocking car felt much more unsteady than Rosa had expected it to, and she swallowed to moisten her parched throat as the carnie operating the ride pulled a rope across their laps to hold them in.

"I've never been on an amusement park ride," Rosa admitted.

Marjorie shot her a look of surprise. "Never in your life? They don't have fairs in London?"

"Not quite like this."

The chair jerked forward, and Rosa held in a gasp. Diego stared up from his spot in the satchel and mewed.

"We'll be all right," Rosa said. A second later, though, their car lifted off, and her stomach dropped out from underneath her. "Oh."

Marjorie laughed. "Don't worry. There's nothing to it. Once it gets going, it's a lot of fun. But you must relax and enjoy the view. Take a few deep breaths."

As a London police officer, Rosa experienced plenty of uncomfortable and dangerous situations. But something about going up, with barely a strap to hold her in, played on her fears.

Once their car reached a steady pace, it jerked less, and she focused on the view. Moments later, as the pier and most of Santa Bonita came into view, her gasp was that of awe. The businesses lining the beach looked like colorful toys on the sand, and the sun sparkling above her seemed close. The whole town felt so much grander than it had before.

As Rosa's carriage reached the top for the second time, she found she was able to watch the roller coaster as it traveled quickly on its course. Impulsively she looked for Victor Boyd, and spotted his dark head at his position at the control platform. Coming up from behind was the unmistakable figure of Joyce's husband, Don, in his bowling shirt, his long legs making fast strides. He towered over Victor, but even from her position above the crowds she could see that the conversation that ensued was unpleasant. Don Welks pointed a long finger in Victor's face, and Victor, who was shorter but beefier, slapped it away. Don Welks stepped back, then pivoted, before marching away.

"Did you see that?" Rosa said as their carriage began its descent.

"See what?" Marjorie asked.

"Victor Boyd and Don Welks were having words."

Marjorie strained her head. "Shoot. I missed it. Was Joyce there?"

"No," Rosa answered, wondering where Don Welks had left his wife. Perhaps in their car, but what had made him so determined to speak to Victor Boyd before leaving?

The ride slowed, pausing carriage by carriage to let the riders off. When they regrouped with the others, Marjorie called out, "Next stop: *tilt-a-whirl*!"

Rosa didn't know what a "tilt-a-whirl" was, but she was pretty confident it would not be a cat-appropriate ride, not that any of the carnies would likely agree to let her on board if they knew what was in her bag.

"I'll watch from the sidelines," Rosa announced. "I've got my kitten with me."

It turned out that Rosa wouldn't see much of the tilt-a-whirl experience from the sidelines as the ride was housed in a large wooden building. Rosa waved when the lineup disappeared inside. It was probably a good idea for her to keep an eye out for Gloria. Where was she? Rosa felt a tickle of worry. Gloria should've made it back from the restaurant by now.

Happy screams erupted from the nearby roller coaster each time it rounded the corner with a new load of riders, and Rosa wondered what thrilling hill or curve lay beyond her vision. Fairgoers passed her with popcorn or cotton candy in their hands, chattering away to each other with smiles on their faces.

The tilt-a-whirl building had patrons exiting, but none were yet her group of friends. The carousel had also stopped and let folks off. The roller coaster rounded the corner for the third time—she'd been counting—when several riders waved their hands at the control platform, presumably to get Victor Boyd's attention.

Why hadn't the ride been stopped? And where was Victor Boyd?

Rosa grabbed Diego's squirmy body and pushed him back into her satchel before hurrying toward the control platform.

What in heaven's name was going on?

4

As the control platform for the roller coaster came into view, Rosa saw that the small square pad that housed the levers and controls for the ride sat empty. The entire upper half of the platform—with only four corner beams running to a metal roof—was open. Had Victor simply walked off with the ride still running?

The roller coaster whooshed past Rosa as she continued to move toward the control platform while Diego did everything in his power to squirm out of her bag. Rosa had no idea how to operate a roller coaster, but she had to do something!

Folks on the runaway ride called out, "Hey!" and "When is this going to stop?"

A young carnie who couldn't have been more than seventeen, ran from around the back of the roller coaster and toward the control platform. The kid wore jeans, a gray T-shirt, a dingy brown apron with tear-off tickets sticking out of the top, and a nametag that read "SKIP".

"What's going on with the coaster?" he said to no one. "Where the heck is Vic?"

Skip unlatched a lock, swung the gate open, and swore. Rosa, having stayed close behind, could see around his back. Victor Boyd was slumped into the bottom half of the small platform.

Skip kicked at Victor's shoes. "Hey, you stoned?"

Rosa stepped around Skip. "Can you stop the ride?"

Skip stared at the controls. "There's some sorta defect." He ran for the wire mesh fence housing the roller coaster, yelling over his shoulder, "Don't touch nothing!" Deftly, he pulled himself over the fence, and flipped open a gray fuse box attached to a post.

As he pulled a lever to stop the roller coaster, Rosa lowered her satchel to the floor. "Stay put," she said to Diego, then turned her attention to Victor. "Victor? Victor Boyd? Can you hear me?"

The chains running along the nearby roller coaster track slowed, and soon the *clack, clack, clack* from the roller coaster grew noticeably slower until it finally came to a stop.

Victor remained unresponsive. His head was turned at an awkward angle, and his unkempt dark hair was mussed over his eyes. Rosa shook him by the shoulders, but he didn't rouse. Reaching for his neck with two fingers, she was vaguely aware of the complaints coming from the roller coaster riders.

Rosa could find no pulse.

Victor Boyd was dead.

"What? What's going on with Vic?" Skip asked, when he returned. "Why'd he pass out?"

Rosa checked her watch and then stood, surveying the situation. She turned to Skip. "You said there was a defect? What did you mean?"

"The train shoulda stopped after two rounds." Skip pointed to the control panel. "See them there black splotches? Looks like burn marks. And the lever shoulda had rubber on it. They all got rubber on them for safety."

Skip kicked at Victor's feet again. "Dude!"

Rosa placed a palm on the carnie's arm and shook her head. "I'm afraid he's dead."

Skip stared back blankly. "What?"

"Skip, I need you to do two things for me, all right?" Rosa forced Skip to look into her eyes. "Report this incident to your manager and tell him to call an ambulance, then immediately go to the bandstand and talk to the lead singer. His name is Detective Belmonte. Tell him Rosa needs him urgently at the roller coaster. Can you do that?"

"Yes, ma'am. Tell Mr. Henderson and fetch a detective." Skip turned and jogged away.

Rosa struggled to close the gate on the control platform again, as one of Victor's legs had wedged into the opening. She didn't want to move his body, but she also couldn't risk having any fair patrons happen upon him in this state. She knew from experience that a dead body would most certainly cause pandemonium.

After nudging Victor's leg almost back onto the platform, Rosa pushed the gate as far as it would go, and just in time. A moment later, a man with angular features stomped toward her. He flailed his arms to the sides and yelled, "What the heck happened with the ride? Where's the carnie? My daughter just got off and threw up, ya know?"

Rosa wasn't about to tell him one ride operator had died, and the ticket-taker had raced for help. Instead, she held her satchel with a squirming Diego in front of her and stood in front of the crack in the gate, hoping to obscure the irate man's vision.

"I'm reporting this to the pier office right now!" He shook a fist in Rosa's direction as though the incident had been her fault.

Rosa called after him, "Yes, you should do that. Right away!" The pier office should know what had just transpired at their roller coaster, and if Skip failed to do as she'd instructed then perhaps this man would bring them the news.

Keeping an eye on Victor Boyd's body, Rosa remained at the control platform. A line had formed on the opposite side with fairgoers oblivious to the hazards of this ride. She hoped none, with their growing impatience, would wander over to find the dead operator.

Two other carnies came by, and Rosa diverted them from getting too close by asking, "Do either of you have a sign that will close the ride temporarily? There's been an accident, and it would be terrific if you could make sure the pier manager knows about it."

The carnies looked at each other, nodded, and then rushed off in the direction they'd come from to grab some signage.

Rosa continued to keep the site quiet. Word getting out would not be good—not for the pier's business, but more importantly—if the news was contained, the police would have a clean and calm scene to investigate. For all Rosa knew, Victor could have died of natural causes, but Skip's mention of a "defect" had her instincts on high alert. Besides, she was trained to treat all deaths as suspicious until they were unquestionably ruled as accidental.

Diego didn't like missing out on the action, it seemed, and before Rosa could stop him, he perched his tiny paws along the top rim of her satchel and launched out of it.

"Diego!"

If he wandered off, Rosa wouldn't be able to leave the body to go after him. But fortunately, her kitten was only interested in a small pool of water that had formed behind the control platform, and began drinking.

Rosa felt a wave of remorse. "I'm sorry, Diego, I should be taking better care of you." Giving her kitten a moment to quench his thirst, Rosa picked him up. She lined her face up with his as if looking him in the eye might help him understand.

"I'll get you another drink, one that's not part of a crime scene, just as soon as I can." Rosa lowered Diego back into her bag. "But for now, it would be best for everyone if you took a little nap."

Just as she looked up, two men rushed at her from different directions. One was Miguel, concern etched on his face, and the other was a pudgy short man, in a wrinkled white shirt and a well-worn hat, who kept a good pace despite his stubby legs and big belly. Rosa had the impression he walked fast wherever he went. His eyebrows pulled together—stern bordering on angry—and as he approached, he called out, "What's going on here? And who are you? What are you doing here?"

When the man moved closer, Rosa saw his nametag: JOE HENDERSON—MANAGER.

At the same time, Miguel called out, "What's wrong, Rosa? I heard you needed my help?"

Rosa looked between them for mere seconds before settling her eyes on Mr. Henderson and delivering the news. As a police officer, she knew Miguel would overhear the information directed at others, and besides, she didn't have time for formal introductions. If they came much closer, they would likely get a visual clue of what had recently transpired.

"I'm afraid there's been an incident," Rosa said to

Mr. Henderson. She'd had the sad experience of relaying news of a loved one's death to relatives or of dead employees to business managers often. One thing she'd learned was that you never knew how the person left behind might react. It was essential to be clear and concise, but with a soft and compassionate tone. "The roller coaster wasn't stopping, and when Skip, the ticket-taker, and I came over to investigate, we found the operator collapsed on the platform."

At her words, Miguel took a few steps forward, and peered over the chest-high ledge into the control platform. His eyes flashed with understanding. Rosa motioned to Miguel as she continued to address Mr. Henderson. "This is Detective Belmonte from the Santa Bonita Police Department. I'm afraid I couldn't find a pulse on the operator. Do you have a first aid attendant on-site?"

Mr. Henderson stepped up to the platform, stared at the body, then stepped away. As if the sight of a corpse was a typical day-to-day affair, his stern expression never wavered. Rosa had to wonder how many of his carnies had collapsed at their posts.

Miguel reached for the gate. "May I?"

He brushed past Rosa before she could step completely out of the way. They paused as if touching had surprised them both, before Miguel took another step and squatted before the body. As he checked for a pulse, Rosa turned back to Mr. Henderson.

"I'm a police officer from London." She shook his

hand. "WPC Rosa Reed. I'm in town on holiday, but I happened to be at the right place at the right time—or the wrong place at the wrong time, I suppose. I've tried to keep the situation as quiet as possible, but a long line of people are waiting to board the roller coaster."

Mr. Henderson grunted.

"I sent a couple of carnies to post a sign," Rosa continued, "but before any of them start asking questions, you may want to say that there's been a technical difficulty, and you're temporarily closing the roller coaster. Do you know if an ambulance has been called?"

Mr. Henderson nodded, a cuss word escaping his lips. "I called for them myself." He reached for a wooden sign behind the door that read, CLOSED FOR MAINTENANCE.

Rosa silently chided herself. If she'd taken a closer look, she could've hung the sign herself. She blamed Diego for distracting her, but when she peered down at his sweet, inquisitive face, her annoyance was short lived.

"Mr. Henderson," Miguel said. "Please make sure the police are called."

The manager snorted, then hurried off as fast as his short legs could take him.

Miguel patted his shirt pockets out of habit but came up empty.

Digging through her satchel, Rosa reached around

Diego's warm, fuzzy body and produced a notebook and pen.

Miguel received it with a look of gratitude. "Thanks." He surveyed the platform as Rosa filled him in on what she knew.

"The body is as I found it. As you can see, there aren't any signs of blood, only some bodily fluid issues." Rosa pointed to the wet spots she had just noticed on Victor's jeans. These reactions were common in the recently deceased. "There appear to be burn marks on the fingers of the right hand."

Miguel glanced up. "Electrocution?"

"That would be my guess," Rosa said. "Skip, a carnie who arrived on the scene at the same time as I did, noticed some blackened marks on the control panel." Rosa pointed to the areas. "And also mentioned the levers are usually covered in rubber for safety."

Only now did Rosa grasp that if Skip hadn't been there to help, she could have quite possibly electrocuted herself. She needed to read up on the technicalities of electricity and electrical engineering.

Miguel glanced up from his notes. "Did you happen to notice the time?"

Rosa tapped her wristwatch. "I found him like this at sixteen forty-eight."

Their gazes locked, and a moment of silence stretched between them. When they had police business to discuss, they were great together, Rosa mused, but then out of nowhere, her heart interfered in the most juvenile way, and, quite inappropriately, she was contemplating how attractive Miguel was when in take-charge mode.

"Rosa?"

"Oh, yes, sorry, my mind drifted." Rosa had to rein in her thoughts! Best to get back to business and the seriousness of the current situation. "What can I do to help?"

"Would you mind going to the bandstand to let my piano player, Terence, know what's happened? My partner, Detective Sanchez, is here somewhere. Ask Terence to find him and send him my way. The band can go on without me or bow out of the second set.

"Would you mind watching Diego? It'll be easier for me to run."

Miguel looked up in surprise. "You brought your cat to the fair?"

Rosa flashed him a wry smile over her shoulder as she rushed away.

5

By the time Rosa had returned to the scene at the roller coaster, yellow rope had been strung up by the police, blocking off the area. People stood in groups, staring and pointing, curious as to why the roller coaster had stopped, some expressing outrage at having paid good money to come to the fair, and how disappointing it was!

Pushing past them, Rosa wondered if Miguel had discovered anything new while she was gone. But Marjorie and her group, who were laughing and obviously not aware of the emergency, intercepted her.

"You missed a neato keeno ride, Rosa!" Marjorie stood between Rosa and Rosa's view of Miguel.

"Oh. Yes. Well . . ." Rosa ducked her head to the side, feeling caught between the need to explain herself to her group of friends and the urge to return to Miguel and the scene.

Nancy followed Rosa's gaze. "What's going on over there?"

Mr. Henderson, marching in his ox-like fashion, was bearing toward Miguel, and Rosa didn't want to miss what the manager had to say. Even though she wasn't officially working with the police department on this case, she was a material witness and couldn't help but feel invested.

"Excuse me," she told Marjorie and Nancy, slipping between them and Pauline.

It occurred to Rosa that while her Aunt Louisa would always introduce Rosa as a police officer, Gloria usually introduced her as her cousin from London. As far as Rosa knew, even Nancy was unaware of Rosa's chosen vocation as they'd stopped writing by the time Rosa had decided to join the force. She left confused whispers in her wake as she rushed toward the yellow rope.

Miguel regarded Rosa with interest as she approached, his warm eyes never failing to cause her heart to flutter. She gritted her teeth, determined to remain professional.

"Detective Sanchez is informing the Chief Medical Examiner and will join us shortly," Rosa said.

Despite Miguel's firm grip, Diego squirmed out of his big hands. "He kept crawling out of your bag."

Rosa grabbed the kitten before he could scurry away, and after a soft reprimand, tucked him back into her satchel. "What have you figured out?" she asked.

"I don't think this death was natural," Miguel said, looking relieved to be off kitten duty. "And I'm not sure it was an accident."

Since Skip had mentioned the missing rubber on the control lever, Rosa's intuition had been the same. "His name is Victor Boyd."

Miguel raised a brow. "I didn't find a name tag or any identification."

"I remember him from school."

The reference to Rosa's time in Santa Bonita during the war was like a shock of electricity between them. Those were the days when Rosa and Miguel had been desperately in love.

Miguel looked away, but Rosa didn't miss how he swallowed.

A flurry of murmurs erupted behind Rosa, and her memories slammed back to the present. By the look on Miguel's face, he seemed back as well. She supposed the onlookers were bound to figure it out soon enough. She just hoped they would keep their voices low so as not to draw too much of a crowd.

"His fingers and hands show signs of burns," Rosa said.

Miguel nodded. "I noticed that too. Fingers blackened and blistered." He called on Mr. Henderson. "Sir, when was the last time you had this equipment inspected?"

"Two days ago!" The manager who had held no variance in expression before this, reddened suddenly.

The creases in his forehead deepened. "I get this equipment checked every week, without fail."

Rosa felt Diego moving around in her satchel, sparking a memory. She still hadn't gotten her kitty a drink of water, but more importantly, she wondered if Miguel had seen any signs of the water Diego had led her to earlier. "Miguel, did you notice any water on the platform?"

Miguel's bottom lip protruded as he shook his head.

Rosa pointed behind the platform. "It looks like it may have leaked out from somewhere inside."

Miguel and Mr. Henderson both leaned over to see the small puddle of water. Victor's left pant leg of his jeans was wet, as well as some of his T-shirt.

Mr. Henderson motioned upward. "We installed steel roofs over all the control panels—so they won't be affected by rain."

They all looked up to the steel roof, but something else caught Rosa's attention.

"What's that bucket for?" she asked. A wooden bucket hung from a handle on one of the rafters.

Mr. Henderson shook his head, his jowls quivering. "That shouldn't be there."

Miguel pushed up on the ledge of the platform and lifted himself until he could get a knee on it, and then a foot. He grasped the corner roof support to pull himself the rest of the way up. He couldn't quite glimpse into the bucket, but he could tip it and get his hand into it.

Miguel held damp fingers to his nose. "It's water. There's a little left in the bottom."

As Miguel moved the bucket back into place, a thin string dangling down from it became visible. Rosa reached for it.

"What's this for?" She studied the frayed end, tugged at it, and immediately saw it was attached to the upper rim of the bucket. The bucket wobbled with the movement, but she could imagine it would take some force to turn it over. Who would come along and tug on a string without looking up to see where it led first?

"Could it be some kind of prank?" Rosa mused aloud.

Miguel hopped down and spoke to Mr. Henderson. "Sir, if you didn't rig a bucket full of water over the roller coaster control panel, who would have done such a thing? Someone who doesn't know that water is a very good conductor of electricity, I'm guessing."

Mr. Henderson's face was beet red. Rosa wondered if smoke would soon swirl from his ears. "I know *exactly* who would have done such an idiotic, brainless thing," he said. "Wait here. I'll get 'im."

It wasn't like they were about to leave, and as it was, Detective Sanchez, dressed in rumpled plain clothes, arrived right at that moment. Rosa had yet to see the man in uniform or in anything properly ironed for that matter. He held a deep-fried carnival pastry in his hand, and an unlit cigarette dangled from his mouth.

Miguel eyed his partner's appearance then got to the point. "I'm treating it as a suspicious death. Don't let anyone near the body."

Detective Sanchez tucked his dead cigarette back into a flattened package. "Dr. Rayburn's on his way," he said before taking a large bite of his pastry.

"I'm going after the pier manager," Miguel said.

"Sure thing, boss," Detective Sanchez said after swallowing. "I'll hold down the fort."

Miguel caught Rosa's eye and motioned with his head in the direction that Mr. Henderson had disappeared. Rosa didn't know if this was an invitation for her to come along, but she took it as one.

It wasn't difficult to find the pier manager. His loud, angry voice carried a long way. He was at the control booth for another ride—one with airplanes moving up, down, and around in circles.

"I can't believe you kids could be so stupid!" Mr. Henderson yelled at a man who must have been at least mid-twenties, despite being called a "kid". The carnie's hair was greased up on the sides with the ends curling into a "jellyroll" meeting at the part. He wore a dirty white T-shirt, and jeans that looked like they were about to wear through in a dozen places.

Mr. Henderson shook a fat finger at the young carnie. "If I've told you once, I've told you a hundred times; there are consequences to your actions."

Miguel interrupted. "Mr. Henderson, might I have a word with your employee?"

Mr. Henderson grunted. "Have at 'er."

The skinny lad had a look of terror on his freckled face.

"I'm Detective Belmonte with the Santa Bonita Police Department," Miguel began. "Can you tell me your name?"

The carnie looked between Miguel and his boss, his face going white. "Wh-why?"

Mr. Henderson held his hands splayed open to the sides as if to say *I told you so.*

"If you don't mind," Miguel said with authority, "just answer the question, please."

"I—Jimmy. Jimmy Thompson." He looked at Mr. Henderson again but just as quickly turned back to Miguel. "Why? What did I do?" Jimmy had the voice of a man who honestly didn't know what he'd done wrong.

Trying not to disturb Diego, who had finally fallen asleep again, Rosa removed a second notepad and pen from her satchel and added Mr. Thompson's name to her notes.

"We're not accusing you of anything, Mr. Thompson," Rosa said, keeping her voice soft. "Can you tell Detective Belmonte how well you knew Victor Boyd?"

Another glance to his boss. "I mean, we worked together, right?" he said, as though he might not know if that was the correct answer. "Me and Vic, we're friends."

"Ha!" Mr. Henderson let out a loud, humorless

laugh. "Do friends puncture each other's tires in the parking lot? Do friends stick maggots in each other's lunch bags?"

Jimmy smiled weakly. Apparently, he didn't know the severity of the situation. "Sure, we like to prank each other some. It's what friends do."

Miguel's jaw tightened and then released. "Mr. Thompson, did you recently rig a bucket of water above the roller coaster control platform?"

Jimmy looked at his boss again. Mr. Henderson nodded with raised eyebrows as though he already knew the answer. "Yeahhh . . ."

"Jimmy Thompson," Miguel said, "I'm going to have to ask you to accompany me to the police station for questioning concerning the death of Victor Boyd."

It took Jimmy several long seconds to process Miguel's words. As Rosa watched the realization dawn that his friend was dead, Mr. Henderson was the next one to speak.

"I can't lose two carnies in one night! How am I going to keep the place running?"

Rosa turned to him, having a hard time grasping his lack of perspective. "Mr. Henderson, at this point, I should think you should feel relieved that the police aren't shutting down the entire boardwalk until they complete this investigation."

Miguel nodded. "Your roller coaster is to remain nonoperational until further notice. As for the rest of the park, I would recommend you keep this incident as quiet as possible."

With that, Rosa and Miguel left Mr. Henderson to deal with the airplane ride and returned to Detective Sanchez at the roller coaster with Jimmy Thompson in tow. The whole time, Jimmy was muttering, "I didn't kill him! I couldn't have killed him."

"Mr. Thompson, please." Rosa placed a finger to her lips. "I recommend that you refrain from speaking until you have a solicitor present."

6

When Rosa and Miguel returned to the scene, Detective Sanchez, along with several policemen who had recently arrived, stood just inside the yellow rope. Taking regular walks to keep the crowd back, Detective Sanchez said, in his usual brash tone, "Keep moving, people. Nothing to see here."

The gate to the control booth now sat open, but there was a large sheet draped over it and the surrounding area to hide what was behind. Two sets of shoes were visible under the sheet, so Rosa assumed a paramedic and perhaps Dr. Rayburn had arrived.

Once they were on the other side of the rope, Miguel had a quick and quiet conversation with Detective Sanchez.

Jimmy still chattered on. "He kicked the bucket? I can't believe it."

It wouldn't take long for Jimmy's unbridled thoughts to cause a stir, but soon Detective Sanchez had him by the arm. "Let's go, Mr. Thompson," he said, leading the poor carnie away.

Miguel cleared his throat to make an announcement to the gathering crowd. "Ladies and gentlemen, if you'll give me your attention for a moment. I'm Detective Miguel Belmonte of the Santa Bonita police. I'd like to put your minds at rest. No one who has ridden on the Sea Viper Roller Coaster tonight has been harmed."

People looked confused by this statement, especially with the yellow rope right in front of them. "However," Miguel continued, "there has been an incident, and one of the boardwalk employees has been hurt. I'd like to ask that you have respect for the injured person and give us some space to work. Please." He motioned around him. "Go on with your night!"

Rosa recognized the police photographer, Officer Richardson, moving around the roped-off area taking photographs. He and Rosa had become acquainted on their previous case, and unfortunately had gotten off on the wrong foot. Rosa was determined to stay out of the churlish officer's way if possible.

Another policeman posted more CLOSED FOR MAINTENANCE signs. Miguel and Rosa both moved toward the white sheet to see if Dr. Rayburn was ready to confirm the cause of death, but as they did, Rosa heard Gloria's loud and boisterous voice.

"Oh, there you are!" she said, walking purposefully toward Rosa. "I'm so sorry I took so long, but the manager of the Lobster Bar and I got to chatting, and well, you know how time flies . . ." The moment she seemed to clue in to the strange scene, Gloria stopped her explanation and stood in place. Their friends, whom Rosa had momentarily forgotten about, stood nearby, whispering behind the roped-off area.

"Gloria!" Marjorie shouted. "You've missed all the excitement." She dropped to a loud whisper. "Victor Boyd is dead!"

Rosa caught Marjorie's gaze with a hard glare. "Shh. The police want to keep this quiet, Marjorie."

Marjorie smirked. "Oh, everyone's talking about it, honey," she said rather loudly, as though she wasn't about to take instruction from Rosa.

"*Ladies!*" Rosa whispered, waving for the four to gather close. "Yes, there's been an unfortunate accident, but we need to keep quiet. The assistant medical examiner is taking a look, and then we'll know more, but the last thing we want is to make a public spectacle."

"Hmph. Not unfortunate, if you ask me," Marjorie said, crossing her arms.

Nancy patted her sister's arm. "We'll keep it down, Rosa. But what's going on?"

"Why are you asking her?" Marjorie said. Then to Rosa, "What makes you the boss here?"

Pauline said nothing, but Rosa could see the question behind her eyes.

Gloria jumped in. "Oh, Rosa is a police officer with the London Metropolitan Police Department."

In unison, the jaws of Marjorie, Nancy, and Pauline dropped and closed again like three stunned fish.

"Y-you're with the police?" Marjorie finally stammered.

Gloria responded proudly, "She's already helped the Santa Bonita Police solve a crime."

Rosa remembered both ladies as young teens, always trying to one-up each other.

"I consulted on one case," Rosa said.

Marjorie murmured to Nancy in a voice that was plenty loud enough for Rosa to hear. "A woman police officer from *London*?"

Her implication was clear: what business did Rosa have inserting herself into police business?

Marjorie had a point, and if Rosa hadn't found the body, she wouldn't have gotten involved.

Pauline, silent as always, had moved to the side, as though she might get a glimpse past the white sheet blocking Dr. Rayburn and Victor Boyd's body.

"Rosa!"

Miguel's voice reached Rosa, and he waved her over.

"Wait a minute," Nancy said. "That's Miguel Belmonte . . ." Her brow raised in question.

Rosa shook her head sharply. "It's professional."

A paramedic made his way out of the roped-off section, followed by Dr. Rayburn, who ducked from behind the white sheet. Rosa, leaving her friend, joined the pathologist and Miguel as they were about to confer. Dr. Rayburn's deep-blue eyes settled on Rosa for a long second.

"Cause of death?" Miguel asked, needing it stated officially.

Dr. Rayburn answered solemnly, "Electrocution is my best guess until I can do the autopsy."

Like the first time Rosa had met Dr. Larry Rayburn, his Texan drawl threw her off. She fought a grin at his every word; after all, this situation demanded seriousness.

"I'd estimate the time of death at about sixteen forty-five," Dr. Rayburn continued, which was only three minutes earlier than Rosa had noted. "The park closes soon."

Rosa was surprised to look at her watch and see it was already near 6:00 p.m.

"I'd like to have my team come and remove the body," Dr. Rayburn continued. "They'll do it as quietly as possible."

Miguel nodded. "I need to get back to the station, question the suspect who looks to be responsible for this incident, and probably book him." Moving aside to one of the policemen, he said, "Be sure to obtain verification of the important elements before you leave here tonight, and stay until they remove the body. We can't count on this remaining a clean crime scene."

While Miguel was busy organizing his officers, Dr. Rayburn raised a blond eyebrow at Rosa and asked, "To what do I owe the pleasure of your presence again, Miss Reed?"

"Please, call me Rosa," she said, feeling her face stupidly blush. "I'm here with friends. I was waiting for them to come off of a ride," she glanced into her satchel at her sleeping kitten, "when I noticed the riders on the roller coaster were in a low level of distress. When I investigated, I found the body."

"Well, Miss Rosa Reed," he drawled, "I must admit, I couldn't have asked for better fortune than Dr. Philpott being off duty today. It is so very nice to see you again."

It seemed odd to be fighting a smile while standing so close to a dead body. Dr. Rayburn must have noticed this too as he touched Rosa's elbow to lead her a few feet away from the control platform.

"Are y'all in town for a while, after all?"

"For a while, certainly," Rosa answered. "I'm not sure when I'm going back to London."

Or if.

Rosa was startled by the thought. Would she actually consider *not* going back? She quickly pushed the thought out of mind.

"Well, if you ever get a hankerin' for the best seafood in town—or hamburger, whatever's your fancy, ma'am—maybe you'd allow me to take ya out to dinner."

Even though the sun was about to set, Rosa suddenly felt much warmer than she had all day.

"Oh, Dr. Rayburn, I—"

"Larry," he said in his warm Texan accent.

Rosa's eyes flitted to Miguel, just for a second, but it was enough to make her realize dinner with Larry might not be such a bad idea. Miguel was engaged to be married, after all, and Larry would be a welcome distraction.

"At least, let me get your number. I was about to head to Galveston, but I'll be stickin' around now with this new case."

"Galveston?" Rosa asked, glad to have the subject on something else so she could catch her breath.

As she looked back at Larry, he nodded. "It's where my family lives. I'm afraid I'm a real mama's boy. Get back there as often as I can. Only goin' for a couple days."

Rosa still had her notebook out, so she scribbled down the Forresters' phone number, tore out the page, and passed it over. Dr. Larry Rayburn was an attractive gentleman. *There's nothing wrong with accepting his invitation to dinner,* she told herself. A weight of guilt still rested on her when it came to the idea of dating.

Just then, Miguel made his way back over. "Officer Richardson will be keeping an eye on everything and taking photos until the park closes," he said to Dr.

Rayburn. "If you wouldn't mind checking in with him before your team leaves . . ."

Dr. Rayburn nodded to Miguel and gave a long look at Rosa before he held up her folded paper, raised his pale eyebrows, and headed off to contact his team.

After Dr. Rayburn had walked away, Miguel turned to Rosa. "Thank you for all of your help tonight. I'm sorry we seem to have disrupted your vacation once again, but hopefully, you can get back to your fun now."

"I was happy to be of service," Rosa said, even though she had no intention of leaving just yet. She hoped to look over the place a little more closely. Something about Victor Boyd's death wasn't sitting right with her. Perhaps it was the regret at not having taken time to have a word with him earlier and letting him know she remembered him and how he'd once come to her defense. Whatever the reason, she didn't feel ready to leave.

Rosa turned to Gloria and the other girls. "Any chance you can catch a ride home with these ladies, Gloria?" she asked. "I might still be a few minutes and poor Diego needs a bit of food and water."

"Sure I can," Gloria said as she reached for the satchel.

"Gloria can ride with me," Marjorie offered as the ladies drifted away. A moment ago, they had been in shock from discovering a dead body at the funfair. Now, it seemed, they had moved on to realizing their high school bully had finally gotten what he deserved.

As Rosa waved goodbye, Terrence, Miguel's bandmate, approached, accompanied by a striking blonde. Styled in large waves, her hair moved as one when she turned her head. She had thick eyelashes, and her bright-pink lipstick matched her shoes and her purse, which looked lovely against a creamy swing dress.

Terrence cocked his head as he stared at Miguel. "I told Charlene what had happened and offered her a ride home, but she insisted on speaking to you first."

Charlene took three quick running steps, tiptoeing toward Miguel on her pink patent-leather T-strap ballroom pumps, and grasped his hand. "Oh, darling. I can't believe what happened. Are you all right?"

Por todos los santos!

Rosa held in a groan. This was Charlene Winters. Gloria's description of her hadn't been far off—she did have a Marilyn Monroe quality. And that explained the gorgeous shoes. Rosa recalled that Miguel's fiancée worked as a receptionist for a shoe company in Los Angeles while hoping to become the next movie star.

Miguel stroked Charlene's hair in a manner that made Rosa's chest tighten.

"All part of the job, sweetheart," he said gently. "I'm just sorry I had to leave you alone all night. Will you forgive me if I find you another ride?"

Charlene pushed out her full lower lip. Miguel, seeing this, changed his mind.

"Actually, I was just leaving for the precinct. I can drop you off at your motel on my way. How does that sound?"

Charlene's face blossomed into a grin, and moments later, they were leaving together hand in hand. Rosa couldn't seem to help the jealousy that shot through her as she watched the leggy blonde—*his fiancée*, she reminded herself—strut off with Miguel.

But for the first time that night, she felt somewhat satisfied that she had given out her phone number.

7

Not long after the medical examiner's team had removed Victor Boyd's body, Officer Richardson finished taking photos with his Busch Pressman camera. The funfair, much darker after sunset, was also much prettier with its colored lights against the night sky. Officer Richardson's gaze met Rosa's, but he didn't offer a smile. He'd made it clear the last time they'd met that he didn't approve of her involvement in Santa Bonita police work.

"You don't have your kitten with you tonight?" Officer Richardson said with a subtle snarl.

Rosa ignored the slight. "I've sent him home early." Her kitten had probably saved her life tonight, and that thought spurred her on to add, "Though I think he earned his keep."

Officer Richardson persisted, "Why are you still here?"

It was a good question. Unlike last time, Miguel hadn't invited her to consult, and Aunt Louisa hadn't interfered by getting the mayor involved. She should've gone home with Gloria, but something undefined created a sense of unease Rosa had learned to pay attention to. Her mother would've called it a hunch.

"I'm almost done," Rosa said, not exactly answering the question.

Studying the scene from all angles, Rosa still couldn't seem to relax. Perhaps it was the regret of not speaking to Victor while he was still alive that ate at her and nothing more.

Officer Richardson was buckling up his camera case when Mr. Henderson dragged a tall wooden ladder through the funfair and toward the roller coaster. It wasn't until he had it under the barricade rope that Rosa realized what he meant to do with it.

Rosa stopped him. "Mr. Henderson! Please desist!"

He looked over with the same agitated frown he'd been sporting all evening.

"What is it now, Miss Reed?"

"This is still a crime scene," Rosa answered. "You'll need to check with Detective Belmonte before touching anything."

"I don't need no trouble, miss," Mr. Henderson said. "I gotta get the park up and runnin' by mornin'. Gotta get that stupid bucket outta there. Don't know what that idiot Jimmy was thinkin'!"

As grumpy as he was, Rosa still felt for him. If the

medical examiner's office was busy, or if any unforeseen bits of information arose while interviewing Jimmy Thompson, it could be a matter of days or even weeks before the roller coaster reopened. If Jimmy Thompson's interview left any doubt about the prank that had killed Victor Boyd, the police would most certainly remove the bucket themselves and check it for fingerprints.

Mr. Henderson placed a foot on the bottom rung of the ladder, which stunned Rosa, and if she could go by Officer Richardson's wide-eyed glare, it dumbfounded him as well.

Officer Richardson spoke up. "Sir, I have to insist that you keep your hands off until you receive permission from Detective Belmonte. If he finds you've tampered with the scene, he's likely to not only shut down this one ride, but your entire funfair, and you could face charges."

Mr. Henderson froze in place, and a long moment later, the policeman's authoritative voice had the desired effect. Mr. Henderson stepped down from the ladder and reached for the metal brace in its middle.

"Why don't you leave that here," Rosa said, a sudden thought coming to her.

Mr. Henderson snorted but moseyed along with his quick, short-legged gait.

"What do you got in mind, Miss Reed?" Officer Richardson asked.

"There's something about that bucket that bothers me. Would you mind if I had a quick look?"

Officer Richardson nodded begrudgingly. Rosa had the feeling he was uncertain about the arrangement Miguel had with her—none—but Rosa wasn't about to enlighten him just yet.

She spotted a long metal pole with a hook on the end leaning up against the fence. She glanced at Officer Richardson. "Is it all right if I touch this?"

"Sure. I've got my photographs. Do you got gloves?"

Rosa had a pair, but she'd left them in the satchel. She held up her bare hands.

Officer Richardson sighed, and removed a pair of rubber gloves from his pocket. "Here. Don't say I never do anything for ya."

Was that a hint of a smile? Perhaps Officer Richardson was warming up to her.

After examining the hooked end and the dangerously sharp tip, Rosa said "Isn't it odd for an item like this to be left out by the fence for anyone to grab?"

"Now that you mention it," Officer Richardson conceded.

With her gloved hands, she held the pole over her head, aimed for the frayed string which hung from the bucket, and sure enough, it just reached.

Had the pole been used in Jimmy's prank? That would be a question for Jimmy. Rosa wondered what the purpose of the hook was, and why it would be near the roller coaster ride.

"I'd like to climb the ladder and have a look," Rosa said. "You don't mind, do you?"

Officer Richardson held an offering hand out toward the ladder. "I suppose I'd get an earful from Belmonte if I did. The power's still off to the ride, so there shouldn't be any danger."

Rosa found it awkward climbing the ladder in a dress—even with a less-than-full crinoline slip—and in heels, even if they were more sensible than the flashy ones Charlene Winters had been wearing.

Blast! Why did she have to think of her?

Rosa shook her head and focused on the task at hand. The last thing she needed was to fall on her bottom and flash her knickers.

She went as high as she dared but still couldn't see inside the bucket. Like Miguel, she reached into the pail to check the water level. She could see by the damp line on her rubber glove that it was still a quarter full, which seemed odd. The bucket must not have fully turned over.

Rosa tested the mechanism by pulling the string. She put some force behind it and nearly lost her footing on the ladder, but the bucket still barely budged. On closer inspection, Rosa could see that a metal beam holding up the roof was in the way.

Strange. Rosa remembered where Diego had found a drink of water near the back edge of the platform—on the side furthest from the controls. She reached up and turned the pail ninety degrees. This time, when she pulled the string, the bucket tipped easily. The bucket was rigged so it could only tilt in one direction—away from the controls.

Speaking immediately to Miguel was crucial. The prank with the water could *not* have caused an electrical malfunction since it didn't dump anywhere near the controls.

Jimmy Thompson's prank had not caused the death of Victor Boyd.

8

The Santa Bonita Police Department looked nothing like Scotland Yard headquarters in London. During the day, the red-clay tile roof and white stucco exterior of the smaller Spanish mission-style building shone brightly under the California sun. Now, in the last wisps of dusk and under a moonlit sky, it had the essence of a holiday resort.

Rosa parked the Bel Air and walked up the palm-tree-lined sidewalk, but when she pulled on the glass front doors of the police station, she was surprised to find them locked. Her mind was on high alert from the evening's events, and she'd been prepared to barge through a busy office to find Miguel. She rapped on the glass door with two knuckles.

There was movement in the office behind the reception counter, and a second later, a young policeman in uniform unlatched the door. She hadn't met this officer, and she wondered if he always worked nights.

"Ma'am? How can I help you?" he asked, opening the door wide to let her inside.

"I'm WPC Rosa Reed, a friend of Detective Belmonte's." Rosa thought her use of the word "friend" was optimistic, but the truth of their relationship status was complicated. "I'm the one who found the body at the boardwalk. I must speak with him as soon as possible—before he finishes his interview," she added.

The policeman locked the door behind them and led her through to the open office area. This section, filled with cubicles, was dimly lit, quiet, and empty of other officers, which was a complete contrast to how it had been in the daytime when she'd been here.

"I believe Detective Belmonte has finished in the interrogation room," the policeman told her. "But please, wait here, and I'll check." He disappeared down the hall where Rosa knew Miguel's private office was.

Only seconds later, the policeman returned with Miguel on his heels.

"You didn't arrest him, did you?" Rosa spouted. The policeman headed down the hall to the reception area, leaving her alone in the cubicle-filled space with Miguel.

Miguel perched on the edge of a desk. "Well, good evening to you too. And, no, I didn't make any arrests. Delvecchio wanted a full report by morning, so I'm working on that and hoping Richardson will have some photos developed for me soon."

Rosa fanned her notebook. "I discovered something before leaving the boardwalk that will exonerate Jimmy Thompson from any manslaughter charges."

As Miguel listened intently, Rosa explained the mechanics of the bucket placement. "I believe someone rigged the bucket to dump when Victor handled a pole with a hook on the end. The bucket could only turn in one direction—away from the control panel and toward the back of the platform. I found the pole out by the roller coaster's fence. I also looked over the control panel closely, and there were no signs of moisture."

Miguel nodded, deep in thought. "Dr. Rayburn said the wet patch on Victor's shirt was water. We can theorize that as he headed out of the back of the platform with this pole, it pulled on the bucket, splashing him as he stepped off. But what was the pole doing there, and how did Jimmy know that Victor would grab it."

"Not sure, we'll have to ask Jimmy. I would guess it's something that's used regularly. Perhaps to clear the track of any debris or unjam the chain drive on the tracks."

Miguel tapped a pen on the desk and looked at Rosa for so long, it bordered on uncomfortable. But when he spoke again, it was clear his mind was still firmly fixed on the case.

"At any rate," he finally said, "it looks like Jimmy didn't even know enough to realize he was innocent."

"It seems so." Rosa cleared her throat. "At the very least, I think it would be prudent to question him again in the morning about the bucket positioning and the pole."

"Agreed."

The overhead light cast shadows under Miguel's eyes, but Rosa thought some of it might be pure fatigue.

"Any chance you'd let me sit in on that?" Rosa asked. She knew her request could step on toes, but she was sincerely interested in what had happened to Victor Boyd.

"Well, since you found the body and key evidence," Miguel said, "I think it only fair to bring you in, once again, as a consultant. If Delvecchio agrees."

Rosa felt a flutter at this seal of approval and unconsciously moved a strand of her chestnut hair back into place. Rather than letting herself bask in this, she changed the subject.

"What was responsible for Victor's electrocution, if not Jimmy's prank?"

Miguel shifted on the desk and twisted his lips in deep thought. "Electrical malfunction?" But even as Miguel said the words, Rosa sensed he didn't believe them. She didn't either.

"The fair manager, Mr. Henderson, insists his regular maintenance is thorough," Rosa said. "And from what I saw from Skip—the carnie who shut off the roller coaster—his employees are trained well.

"Mr. Henderson is eager to get the roller coaster up and running again," Rosa continued. "He wants to get his electrician in first thing tomorrow to look over the roller coaster control panel. Perhaps you should let him."

Miguel nodded, still clearly in thought. "I'd like to get an independent electrician at the same time."

Rosa awoke the next morning to a loud shriek. "What is this *thing* doing in my living room?"

Pushing herself to a sitting position, Rosa let out a weary sigh. With less grace than an orangutan, she wrestled herself into her silk housecoat, did a desperate search for her slippers, and headed for the stairs to face her angry aunt. *What has Diego done to upset her now?*

"I'm sorry, I'm sorry!" Rosa called the moment she reached the bottom of the stairs. The Forrester mansion was a sprawling, two-level estate with many rooms and corridors. The yards, both front and back, were an impressive display of west coast gardening expertise with fragrant flowerbeds, elaborate water fountains, and manicured hedges.

Rosa raced for the living room situated in the west wing and practically skidded along the hardwood floors. Standing about the slate-blue, low-back Scandinavian-designed couch were her stern-faced aunt and her cousin Clarence, who attempted but failed at hiding his amusement. His little girl, Julie, squealed with delight, her blond ringlets bobbing as she skipped over the yellow area rug.

Diego's sharp front claws had pierced Louisa's heavy front room drapes—yellow, embossed with a white geometrical pattern—and the kitten hung from them like an acrobat. With one paw, he stroked the air trying to catch the curtain's pull string. Even at the height of mischievousness, he was simply adorable!

Clearly, Aunt Louisa didn't see it that way. Impeccably dressed in a striped pencil skirt, and her short brunette hair neatly styled around her ears, Rosa's aunt crossed her arms. A hard frown etched her tanned and make-up-adorned face.

Wearing slacks and a light cotton shirt, Clarence removed a paperback book—a James A. Michener novel—from his back pocket and tossed it onto the glass coffee table before lowering himself into an armchair. He casually crossed his legs, and chuckled. Julie giggled in turn.

Rosa shot her cousin a look that said, *You're not helping!*

"I'm sorry!" Rosa said again as she raced across the room, the hem of her housecoat flapping. She grabbed Diego firmly by the scruff of the neck with one hand and used her other hand to push the middle of his front paws one at a time until his claws released. When she had him cleared of the drapes, she scrutinized the fabric, and sure enough, there were two arcs of tiny holes left behind.

With a sheepish glance toward her aunt, she said, "I'll be happy to replace them."

But as expected, Aunt Louisa huffed out a breath of despair. "They're irreplaceable! They're from Venezuela." Rosa held in a breath of exasperation. All her aunt's home furnishings seemed to be imported from some distant land, and they were all irreplaceable.

"I'm really sorry, Auntie," Rosa said, for what felt like the hundredth time.

"Can I play with him?" Julie tugged on Rosa's housecoat. If anyone could defuse the tension it would be her aunt's little granddaughter.

"Of course you can," Rosa said. "Perhaps you can take him to the nursery?"

Julie awkwardly carried Diego, who looked rather annoyed at having his fun cut short, out of the room. Clarence smirked at Rosa as he followed his daughter. Being divorced, Clarence only had Julie on select days of the week, and Rosa was quite pleased that today was one of them.

Rosa tried another angle of appeasement. "I heard there's a training school for cats in town."

Aunt Louisa's arms remained firmly crossed over her chest. "Cats can't be trained."

"That's not true," Rosa said. "I've read about cats learning to walk on a leash and to enjoy driving in cars. There was a story about that in the *Readers Digest*."

Aunt Louisa harrumphed and strode to the living room door. She paused, and said, "Are you joining us for breakfast?"

It was an unnecessary inquiry, and Rosa took it for an olive branch. "Yes, I am."

After taking time to dress properly, Rosa joined Aunt Louisa in the morning room and took a seat at the table.

Her aunt glanced up briefly with a begrudging look behind her eyes, then flipped open the morning newspaper. "I have a good mind to take that creature down to the ocean and tie a rock to him," she said, her capacity to nurse a grudge on full display.

Rosa failed to rein in her disgust. "Oh, Aunt Louisa! He's just a kitten."

"In my books, that's just another word for a large rat."

Señora Gomez, the long-time housekeeper who wore a perpetual smile, appeared from the kitchen with a platter filled with freshly baked muffins and a small silver coffee carafe, Aunt Louisa's usual breakfast.

"*Buenos días*, Rosa!"

"*Buenos días*, Señora Gomez."

Determined to make amends somehow, Rosa turned back to her aunt. "I thought Diego was with Gloria." A waft of sweet buttery muffin aroma hit Rosa's nose, and she had to help herself to one. They were still warm. "I didn't get home until the wee hours of the morning. It won't happen again." At least Rosa hoped it wouldn't.

Her step-grandmother, Sally Hartigan, made her way slowly from the back hallway, thankfully breaking the uncomfortable silence. Her floral dress hung over soft curves, and a slight bend of her back along with her gray hair twisted into a bun at the nape of her neck attested to her senior years.

Rosa smiled. "Good morning, Grandma Sally."

"Good morning," Grandma Sally returned. Her accent hinted at her many years living in Boston. To Aunt Louisa she said, "Why are we so sour-faced so early in the morning?"

Rosa groaned inwardly, not wanting to hash out her aunt's grievances with little Diego again, but it turned out that Aunt Louisa didn't want to do that either. She sipped her coffee and spoke over the rim. "Only bad news in the paper, as usual. There was a death at the boardwalk last night."

Grandma Sally shot Rosa a conspiratorial look. "Gloria said you were out with that police detective until late last night."

Wanting to avoid the subject of *that police detective*, Rosa asked, "Gloria's up already?"

Grandma Sally poured herself a cup of coffee. "Up with the birds and already gone."

Wow, Rosa thought. *Where had Gloria rushed off to so early?*

Aunt Louisa tapped the newspaper with a long

finger dressed in diamonds. "Wait, Rosa, you already know about this?"

"Gloria and I were at the fair last night. She didn't tell you?"

"That girl never tells me anything, and it appears you don't either."

Rosa felt that judgment was particularly unfair. "I've hardly had a chance to."

Aunt Louisa waved a dismissive hand. "You can tell me now. And please don't dillydally. I have a full day."

Rosa had no intention of dillydallying. Miguel would be meeting the two electricians at the boardwalk soon and hopefully discover the problem with the control panel. He'd want to wrap up his investigation before the park opened, and she didn't want to miss it. She concisely relayed what she knew.

"One of the carnies had an accident of some sort. Sadly, he passed away."

"I know that part already," Aunt Louisa said. "It's in the paper. Do you know how he died?"

Rosa wasn't at liberty to say and used the moment to take a bite of her muffin.

Aunt Louisa was undaunted. "Who was it then? Surely, you must know that."

"Why do you assume that, Louisa?" Grandma Sally said.

Aunt Louisa paused. "I thought you said that Gloria mentioned a *detective*?"

The subject of Detective Belmonte was a sour point between Rosa and her aunt, and it seemed that eleven years hadn't been long enough to erase strong feelings.

"As it turns out," Rosa said, wanting to meet her aunt halfway, "I discovered the body. It was a fellow I went to school with when I lived here. Victor Boyd."

Aunt Louisa stared at Rosa blankly, and Rosa wasn't surprised her aunt hadn't heard of Victor or his family. He was most definitely from the "other side of the tracks".

"Wait," Rosa said with a new thought. "Did Gloria take the Bel Air?"

"I would think so," Aunt Louisa said. She prattled on about needing to get Clarence to take that vehicle into the shop.

Rosa finished her muffin as she stared out the open patio doors. The gardens, a well organized and manicured display of color, sprawled out like a vibrant quilt. A man with dark skin, black hair, and a thin black mustache pushed a wheelbarrow across the lawn.

"Bernardo?" Rosa said. The groundsman had worked for the Forresters in the forties when Rosa had lived there. "He still works here?"

"Of course," Aunt Louisa said.

"Why haven't I seen him before now?"

"His mother was sick. I gave him some time off."

Rosa left her breakfast unfinished, wiped her

mouth with the cloth napkin, and pushed away from the table. "I have to go and say hello."

Bernardo Diaz broke into a toothy smile when he saw Rosa stroll toward him. "Miss Rosa? Is that you?"

Rosa took the man's rough hands in hers. "It is. It's so wonderful to see you again. How's your family?"

"*Muy bien, gracias.* My mother was ill, but is feeling better today."

"And the children?"

"They are all grown as you are, Miss Rosa. I have five grandchildren." Bernardo's dark eyes were bright with pride.

"Well, you're doing a very good job keeping the gardens looking beautiful."

"Mrs. Forrester lets me hire help. My family is very grateful."

Rosa understood. Many of the workers she saw on the peripheral were family members of Señora Gomez and Bernardo. Aunt Louisa had a heart after all.

"Are you staying long, Miss Rosa?"

Rosa hesitated. "I don't really know, Bernardo."

"I hope you can stay for a long time." Bernardo's smile was infectious. Rosa smiled in return.

"Perhaps, Bernardo, perhaps."

9

Since Gloria had absconded with the one vehicle Rosa had permission to use, she had no choice but to ride her bicycle, the Schwinn Deluxe Hollywood, to the boardwalk. She'd taken time to change into a more suitable outfit of capri pants—blue with white stripes—a blue blouse with three-quarter length sleeves, and a pair of white tennis shoes. She didn't fail to attend to her appearance, applying eye make up and a layer of lipstick. Even though Rosa wouldn't admit it to anyone, she couldn't completely put Miguel, and her unrequited feelings that stubbornly remained, out of mind. After brushing her chestnut curls into submission and pinning them behind her ears, she added a cute little sun hat adorned with a blue and white ribbon to her head.

With Diego in the doghouse, so to speak—Clarence had taken Julie back to her mother, Gloria was out, and Señora Gomez had gone shopping, leaving no kitty-sitters about—Rosa brought him along to ride in the satchel in the handlebar basket. As she had boldly pronounced to Aunt Louisa, her kitten really did seem to enjoy traveling, and Rosa was grateful for his adventurous personality.

Miguel was at the gated and locked entrance to the fair when Rosa arrived. Leaning against his unmarked police car, he wore navy pants, a baby-blue cotton shirt with a black tie, and a straw fedora. Rosa couldn't help but think he looked very debonair.

Miguel motioned to her wriggling satchel. "We're involving Deputy Diego again today, are we?" Miguel had been joking about deputizing her kitten since the day she had rescued him from behind the bakery. She liked the sound of his new nickname.

"Well, Deputy Diego *was* the bright officer who helped me discover the mechanics of Jimmy's pail last night," Rosa said with a smile, remembering how a thirsty Diego had led her to the puddle of water. "So, you never know how helpful he might be."

Miguel smirked, producing an extremely distracting dimple, then turned his attention to the metal fence. "I wish I could put Sanchez in a bag like that and take him out only when I need him." He called between the bars of the gate, "Hello? Mr. Henderson?"

The portly man appeared from the direction of the

amusement rides and, with quick, short-legged steps, made his way to the gate.

After polite greetings, Miguel asked, "Have the electricians arrived?"

Mr. Henderson nodded. "Was all I could do to keep 'em from opening the panel until you got here."

Rosa was impressed at how well Mr. Henderson had kept to the police's instructions. He added, "I need to get that ride back up and running by nine."

Mr. Henderson unlocked the gate, then locked it again after Rosa and Miguel crossed through. They followed the manager through the quiet and empty carnival tents—rather eerie without a mass of happy attendees—and onto the amusement ride platform. Once they passed the building that housed the tilt-a-whirl, they could see two men waiting near the roped-off area that held the control platform for the roller coaster. One wore blue work overalls, and the other was in jeans and a grease-marked white T-shirt. Rosa wondered which of them was the regular electrician at the boardwalk and which was the electrician Miguel had hired.

Her question was quickly answered when Miguel strode straight for the man in the blue overalls and thrust out a hand. "Mr. Keenan, I'm glad you could make it on such short notice."

"No problem, Detective, but I have another appointment in a half-hour, so it'll have to be a quick assessment for now."

"Hopefully, that's all it will take anyway," Miguel said.

"Can we finally have a look at this problem you're having?" the man in the stained white T-shirt asked. "I seen some scorch marks on the panel. Sure hope someone wasn't messin' around with it."

"Mr. Keenan, would you mind having a look at the panel?" Miguel's authoritative tone left no room for discussion. He held up the barrier rope for the electrician to duck under. Lifting a small metal toolkit from the ground, Mr. Keenan stepped through the open gate and onto the control platform.

"Power's off at the source?" he asked

Mr. Henderson confirmed that it was.

Mr. Keenan stopped at the main lever, inspecting it from all sides. "Does this not have a rubberized sheath?"

Mr. Henderson moved closer. "It should." He looked to his electrician, who nodded his head.

"Yeah, it should. Did on Tuesday, a red one."

Though he said the words, it seemed to Rosa that the electrician didn't sound entirely certain. When Skip mentioned the missing rubber sheath, Rosa hadn't thought much of it. But if it had been so recently removed, perhaps its absence was more important than she had thought.

Mr. Keenan removed the control panel cover with a small screwdriver to reveal a mass of twisted multicolored wires. With his finger, he followed each wire, one by one, along their paths and nodded at their output below.

Diego stirred, and Rosa tucked a hand into the satchel to scratch him under the chin. Her spoiled pet immediately purred.

Mr. Keenan opened a second panel, a smaller one underneath the first, and drew in a hissing breath. "Who in God's name would connect a live wire to that box?" He shook his head with wide, unbelieving eyes.

"What's that?" Miguel asked.

"This live wire here. The thing's been routed to the metal and taped here like some fool was trying to kill somebody. Metal woulda conducted the electricity through anyone stupid enough to pull on that there power lever."

"How could this have happened?" Mr. Henderson stared at his electrician accusingly.

"I—I dunno," the man said. "I wouldna have . . . I never coulda . . ." He ran a hand over his balding head. Finally, as though he'd found an answer he said, "Couldn'ta been me!"

With everyone staring at him, he explained. "I haven't been in the park for three days. I test all the equipment real careful."

Mr. Henderson started to interrupt him, but before he could, the electrician slammed his hands on the ledge.

"But even if I missed somethin'. Even if I missed *this,*" he said, as though overlooking the wiring were akin to ignoring a horse swimming laps at the local pool. "Even if I was that stupid, it woulda electrocuted your operator the very next time he pulled the lever. It wouldna taken three days!"

"Guy's right," Mr. Keenan said. "This panel was obviously tampered with between the time when your guy stopped the last roller coaster ride an' the time when he started the thing up again."

10

"So, all we have to do is list every single person who was at the fair that night and bring them in for questioning," Miguel said sarcastically as he tapped his pen on his desk. Rosa occupied one of the wooden chairs in Miguel's office, while Diego sniffed every inch of the floor, around filing cabinets, and right up to the frosted glass walls like a tiny feline bloodhound.

"Pick off all the individual strands of hay until we find the proverbial needle," Rosa said. It did seem like a mountain of a case now.

Chief Delvecchio opened Miguel's wooden-veneer door without knocking. "Are you booking the Thompson kid? He's in there whining about how he didn't mean to do it. Seems like a pretty clear-cut case to me."

If only it were that easy, Rosa mused. In fact, the

two electricians had proved without a doubt that Jimmy's prank had not been responsible for Victor's death.

Miguel shook his head at his boss. "It seems we've come up with some new evidence. Rosa was the one to discover it. The water wasn't the conductor that caused the electrical current that killed Victor Boyd."

"What on earth did, then?"

"The electrical panel was sabotaged. The death was premeditated."

"Damn!"

Miguel rose to his feet. "I'll go release Jimmy Thompson right away."

Rosa lifted a finger. "Might I suggest further questioning before you release him?"

In contrast to the resort-like appearance of the outside of the building, the interrogation rooms seemed to come in a one-size-fits-all model—square, with a small table against one wall, and two chairs on either side. Jimmy was seated and waiting.

Once Rosa had explained what she wanted to do, Miguel agreed to let her go in alone. Watching through the two-way glass behind her, Miguel would listen intently while cat-sitting Diego.

"Hi, Mr. Thompson," Rosa said as she closed the door behind her. "Do you remember me from last night? I'm WPC Reed from the London Metropolitan Police working as a consultant for the Santa Bonita police."

Jimmy scanned Rosa's summery outfit. "You don't look like the fuzz."

Rosa removed her sunhat and tapped her temple. "What's important is what's in here, Mr. Thompson." She'd brought along a bottle of soda and now set it in front of him in hopes it would help him to relax. "I have some good news, Mr. Thompson. Upon further investigation, it turns out that we don't believe your water bucket prank was responsible for Victor Boyd's death."

Jimmy blinked once, then twice, and then he quickly scrambled to stand. "So, I can split?"

Rosa held up a palm. "Hold on a minute, Mr. Thompson. Please remain seated. Give me a moment. I promise this won't take long. Enjoy your drink." She motioned to the soda.

Jimmy considered it and then dropped into his chair and took a large swig. "But I can split after this, right?" he asked, ineffectively suppressing a belch. "Or do I need to get that lawyer back in here."

"No need for a lawyer, I assure you. I just think you may be able to help us figure out what really happened to Mr. Boyd. You're a conscientious citizen, Mr. Thompson. You'd like to help us solve this, wouldn't you?"

Jimmy Thompson didn't seem confident about Rosa's verbal assessment but had the sense not to contradict it.

"Sure. Don't know how I can help, though."

"I'm correct in stating that Mr. Boyd was your friend?"

"Yeah," Jimmy started tentatively. "Me and Vic worked together at the park for almost six months." Jimmy's lips pulled up into a nostalgic smile, and Rosa felt bad that he had been held all night, believing he'd accidentally killed his friend. "And the pranks didn't mean nothin'," he added. "It was all in fun."

"Yes, I understand that, and it's unfortunate what happened to your friend." Rosa felt sad about any death—high school bully or not. "Do you know of anyone who may have disliked Victor?" Rosa's mind immediately went to her school friends Nancy, Joyce, and Pauline, along with Gloria and Marjorie. But they wouldn't be the only ones who'd disliked the man. The list would be long.

Jimmy confirmed her thoughts.

"Sure, yeah. Lots of folk didn't have time for Vic. He ticked people off. The guy didn't know how to be friendly sometimes, but—" Understanding bloomed on Jimmy's face. "Wait. Did someone do this to Vic on purpose? Did someone kill him?"

Rosa kept her expression blank. She didn't want Jimmy Thompson blabbing the details all over town, but at the same time, if she wanted to get clear answers out of him, she probably needed to tell him the truth. "That's what it's looking like right now. Yes."

Jimmy slapped his thigh. "Mr. Henderson! I bet he did it. Guy told everyone he was gonna fire Vic."

"Why?"

A shrug was followed by, "I dunno, but if you ask me, the guy was scared of Vic."

Rosa tilted her head. "Why was Mr. Henderson afraid of one of his employees?"

"Vic was always sayin' no to Mr. Henderson, no matter what he asked. He told 'im if he fired him, he'd have a lawsuit on his hands. Don't think Vic knew much about the law, but he had this way of threatenin' people. Ya always believed him."

Mr. Henderson was on the list of suspects, and now they had motive, but Rosa didn't want to stop there. "Is there anyone else you can think of that might have wanted to see Victor, er, out of the way?"

Jimmy lifted a narrow shoulder. "Coulda been anybody, but I'm telling you, Henderson's your man."

Rosa changed tracks. "Who had access to the control panel that operated the roller coaster?"

"Just whoever was on shift. Vic didn't let nobody up on the platform with him if that's what you're askin'."

"Right, but would there have been a time when Mr. Boyd wasn't at his control panel? Is there a time when ride operators aren't at their controls?"

Jimmy slurped his soda. "Well, sure. When we go for a break or let the folks onto the rides. Vic's got it—had it—rough, operating the coaster. Had to make sure each person was buckled right. The airplanes, which I run," he went on, "they only got a rope that swings over their heads. Only takes me 'bout a minute to get all ten people loaded on."

"And the roller coaster held, what, thirty?" Rosa had counted the cars and then calculated the maximum number of passengers before leaving the park the evening before, so she knew this was true before she asked.

Jimmy nodded. "Yes, ma'am."

"And so buckling each of thirty people in individually, that would have taken, what, four or five minutes?"

"More like ten!"

Would ten minutes have been long enough to reconfigure an electrical panel? The power would have surely had to have been shut off first and then turned back on at the very least.

"There was a long pole, maybe seven feet long, with a hook on the end. Any idea what that was used for?"

"The snatch hook? Sure, we all got one at our rides. Stupid idiots throw cups and popcorn boxes from the rides sometimes. There's almost always a mess to clean up when we get back from break. We gotta use the snatch hook to get the junk outta the way."

Rosa slid her notebook toward herself and wrote: *Snatch Hook.* "And did you use Victor's snatch hook to rig the bucket of water?"

Jimmy nodded and looked like he was ready to laugh, but then he remembered the situation and stopped himself. "I knew Vic would have to use it sometime during the day, and he's always annoyed when he does it. Grabs that thing like it's his worst enemy's neck. So, yeah. I had the idea to tie the bucket to it. Figured if I used a thin string, he wouldn't notice nothin'." After a pause, he added. "Guess he didn't." Jimmy's emotions were as easy to read as a small child's. He looked sad, and Rosa wondered how long it would take him to get over the fact that he'd been suspected of killing his friend.

"You've been more than helpful, Mr. Thompson. Thank you. You can go now."

Jimmy drained his soda in one last long gulp then slapped the empty bottle down onto the table. "But if I were you, I'd spend my time looking at Henderson." He pointed at Rosa. "Trust me on this one."

BACK IN MIGUEL'S OFFICE, Rosa slumped into a chair across from Miguel who sat at his desk. Past the point of purring, Diego was curled up in Miguel's arm, fast asleep. Rosa kept her eyes on her notebook because the sight of an attractive police officer cradling a sleeping kitten was simply far too adorable. Especially *this* police officer and this kitten.

"So, we're back to listing every single person either of us recognized at the boardwalk," she said.

"We both know people who had the motive to kill

Victor Boyd," Miguel said in a soft voice as if not to awaken Diego.

Rosa could probably have mentioned that Diego slept soundly through everything from Ferris wheel rides to her raging aunt, but she enjoyed Miguel's soft tone too much to do that.

"But who had the means?" he continued. "Who at the fair would have had the rewiring know-how to instigate the murder?"

Rosa shook her head. "I'm afraid that doesn't eliminate any of the girls from my group of friends. When I was in school, we all worked at the aircraft plant together. I wasn't as skilled at rewiring as some of the others. Joyce was especially skilled. I'm not from this town, and even I know a handful of people who had motive and the means to do this." Rosa tapped her pen on her notepad. She had already listed Marjorie, Nancy, Pauline, and Joyce. They had all known and hated Victor, but Joyce had left before Victor had died. However—

"Don Welks," Rosa said.

Miguel raised a brow. "Huh?"

"From the top of the Ferris wheel, I saw Don Welks—that's Joyce Welks's husband—speaking with Victor Boyd. The conversation was short, but it didn't appear too friendly."

"Are you sure? From that distance, it would be easy to get a fella mixed up."

"Mr. Welks is an extremely tall man," Rosa said.

"Head and shoulders above everyone else, and he wore a distinctive bowling shirt."

Miguel hummed. "Worth checking into the guy."

Rosa added Don Welks to her list, then drew a question mark beside Pauline's name.

"All the girls in the higher grades worked at the aircraft plant, except Pauline. She worked with her dad throughout the war, so I have no idea about her electrical wiring know-how."

Miguel motioned to Rosa's notebook. "Why don't we start with your list and go from there? Even if none of them are guilty, our inquiries could lead us in the right direction."

"Yes, one must start with what one has," Rosa murmured. It was what her father, Basil Reed, had often said while working as a chief inspector for Scotland Yard.

Miguel smiled, both dimples making an unnerving appearance. "You sound so very British when you talk like that."

Rosa straightened. "Like what?"

"Like the Queen. 'One must—'"

"*Pfft*," Rosa protested. "How would you know? When did you ever talk to the Queen?"

"I haven't. She hasn't seen fit to include our little pueblo in her holiday plans so far, but I have seen newsreels. You talk just like her."

Rosa didn't know if she should take that as a compliment or not. "Well, you talk like Desi Arnaz."

"He's Cuban!" Miguel feigned a look of shock, but a slight smile teased his lips.

"Oh, right. Sorry about that." Rosa grimaced at her mistake. Not everyone who spoke Spanish in America came from Mexico. "Yes, well, I *am* very British, and I shan't apologize for that."

Their eyes locked. The eleven years since Rosa had lived in Santa Bonita—sounding very American by the end of it—stretched between them.

"I'd never ask you to," Miguel answered softly. He cleared his throat, and his dimples disappeared. "I see that Gloria is not on your list—"

Rosa's head snapped up.

"It's just a matter of form," Miguel added quickly. "She *was* part of the grouping at the fair that night. I'm just suggesting that you not reveal details if you decide to ask her questions."

Reluctantly, Rosa added Gloria's name to her list. "I think we can quickly clear Gloria. She wasn't even on the boardwalk when the rigging or the death occurred. She'd gone to the Lobster Bar to use the facilities and got caught up chatting with the manager there."

With his free hand, Miguel stopped petting Diego and scrawled "Gloria" and "Lobster Bar" on the notepad in front of him. "I'll follow up on this one and see what I can find out about the other employees at the fair."

Rosa hated that Gloria was officially a suspect, but

she figured the sooner Miguel investigated her alibi, the sooner the police would clear Gloria from suspicion.

"And that's everyone you knew at the boardwalk that night?" Miguel asked in confirmation.

Rosa nodded as she stood and reached for her kitten. Miguel handed Diego over, then with a look of resigned determination said, "Thanks again for your help, Rosa. Please do continue on with what remains of your vacation."

It sounded like a dismissal.

Rosa wasn't about to be dismissed.

11

Diego, however, had other plans. Wriggling out of Rosa's arms he sprinted out of Miguel's office and down the hallway toward the front door.

"Diego!"

Rosa grabbed her hat and satchel and made a run after her cat, flushing with acute embarrassment as the policemen stared, some with mirth pulling on the corner of their lips and others with looks of derision, clearly disapproving of Rosa's decision to bring a cat with her to the precinct, or possibly they disliked that Rosa came in at all.

She slowed her jog and lowered her voice. "*Diego!*"

Miguel dashed past her, leaving a waft of musky cologne in his wake, but just as he was about to reach her cat, someone from the outside opened the door, and Diego slipped out.

Rosa no longer cared that she was being watched and judged, and broke into a run. If Diego decided to climb one of those palm trees, Rosa had no idea how she would ever get him down.

Pushing through the entrance into the bright sunlight, she prepared herself for the worst.

She scanned the treetops. "Where is he?"

Miguel shoved two fists into his pockets and grinned. "I think he wants to go home."

Rosa followed Miguel's gaze to her Schwinn bicycle. Diego sat in the handlebar basket, licking one of his paws as if he hadn't a care in the world.

Rosa let out a breath of relief that turned into a nervous giggle. She slapped a palm over her mouth, feeling like a complete failure when it came to police professionalism. After a moment, she straightened her shoulders and walked as casually as she could to her bicycle. Lifting Diego, she placed him into her satchel and then put the satchel into the handlebar basket. Dratted Miguel hadn't yet gone back inside, but instead he leaned against a palm tree as he watched her with interest.

"Don't you have work to do?" Rosa asked.

"Oh, yes." Miguel pushed off the palm with one foot. "I'd forgotten that cat rescue belongs to the domain of firemen. Good day, Rosa."

Rosa swallowed her humiliation and pressed down on one pedal, launching her bicycle onto the sidewalk.

"I'm taking you home, Diego," she said with a

reproachful tone. "And if you're not careful, I'm going to take away your deputy badge."

Diego poked his head out of the satchel, meowed, then turned his back on her, like he was a prince and she was the hired hand.

Once back at the Forrester mansion, Rosa deposited Diego into Señora Gomez's care in the kitchen. With a shake of her finger she said, "I'm still mad at you."

"Oh, Miss Reed," Señora Gomez said as she poured a bit of milk into a small bowl and placed it on the terra-cotta tiled floor. "What did Señor Diego do?"

Rosa relayed her story and Señora Gomez laughed, wiping a tear from her eyes. "I wish I could've been a fly on the wall."

For the first time since it happened, Rosa smiled. "I suppose it was a bit humorous." A little time and distance had a way of putting things in perspective. Being the laughingstock of the entire Santa Bonita police department wasn't the end of the world.

Right?

Leaving Diego to his snack—Señora Gomez had produced a bit of tuna—Rosa grabbed an apple then headed through the house and up the long flight of stairs to her bedroom.

The room looked much the same as it did when Rosa had occupied it in the early forties. A canopy bed sat against the wall in the center of the room, its oak head and footboards carved ornately and matching the dresser, night tables, and a vanity desk that had an oval mirror and padded stool.

Dark curtains hung on square windows that overlooked the tennis court and a kidney-shaped pool. Besides her clothes, which she'd brought from England and a few pieces purchased in town since her arrival, Rosa had very few personal items. The stack of books that sat on one night table were a selection of novels she'd picked from the Forrester mansion library. Rosa ran a finger along the spines: the latest volumes from C.S. Lewis, Agatha Christie, and Erle Stanley Gardner. Rosa suspected Clarence was behind keeping the family library updated, but it was largely a collection of fiction, and what Rosa needed now was non-fiction, particularly on the subject of electricity.

Though Rosa had a basic understanding of how electricity worked, it bothered her that she didn't understand exactly how the mechanics of the sabotage at the roller coaster ride had been executed. Her work at the aircraft plant had been basic at best.

Getting more detailed information required obtaining specialized textbooks on electrical engineering, not something the local bookstore would carry. No, if Rosa wanted to find comprehensive resources on the subject, she'd have to visit the local library.

The thought of that excursion made Rosa's blood cool. She flopped onto the bed with a bout of lightheadedness. Coming to America was meant to be a break from emotional memories. Rosa had envisioned herself lounging about the pool reading books and eating meals that contained pineapple and coconut. Long walks along the beach with the waves crashing loudly enough to block out her thoughts about Winston, who must be fuming with anger toward her now, and poor Vivien whose grave she hadn't visited in almost a year.

Miguel Belmonte had to ruin it for her. Drat that man!

Rosa heaved herself off her bed with a long sigh. There was nothing stopping her from doing what she'd come to do. She didn't have to involve herself in this latest case. She barely knew Victor Boyd, and Miguel was perfectly capable of solving the case himself. Surely, he'd been able to do his job respectably before Rosa arrived.

She'd stay out of this one, that was what she'd do. Plucking *The Lion the Witch and the Wardrobe* out of the pile—one couldn't get further from a blasted murder mystery than that—Rosa swapped her tennis shoes for sandals and skipped down the stairs in the direction of the pool. In America she wasn't a police officer. She was just a girl on holiday! Surely Señora Gomez would make her a fruit salad with lots of fresh pineapple and coconut if she asked.

Just as she hit the landing, Rosa heard unfamiliar voices coming from the living room. Forgetting momentarily that she was a *girl on holiday!* she took it upon herself to investigate.

A quick peek revealed Grandma Sally drinking tea and watching television, which explained the sounds. Clarence occupied one of the chairs, an ankle braced over his knee.

Rosa announced her presence. "Hiya. What are you watching?"

Grandma Sally waved to the image on the black-and-white television. "*The Edge of Night*. Have you seen this show? I wouldn't start if I were you. Silly nonsense, but tremendously addictive. I just can't stop watching."

Clarence straightened, his face flushing with embarrassment. "I'm just keeping Grandma company. I don't really pay attention to these kinds of shows."

"Come on, now," Grandma Sally said. "You like the mystery elements."

"Yeah, sure, but the romance is a bit thick."

A Pillsbury commercial for instant mashed potatoes flashed across the screen. A stylish housewife in a crisp apron served her husband a dinner plate then winked at the camera. "Nothing says lovin' like something from the oven, and Pillsbury does it best!"

Grandma Sally patted the spot beside her. "You're welcome to join us, Rosa, if you like."

"Maybe another time," Rosa said. "I'm headed out to the pool to read." She lifted her book as if she needed to provide proof.

The episode started playing again, and despite Clarence's protestations of being uninterested, his actions declared otherwise, and his brow furrowed as he focused on the black-and-white images.

Rosa was pleasantly surprised to find Gloria poolside wearing a flouncy pool dress that was opened at the front showing off a red one-piece bathing suit.

She peered at Rosa over a pair of cat-eye sunglasses. "Hiya!" she said as though they hadn't seen each other in a year. "Where ya been?"

"I could ask you the same thing." Rosa reclined in a cedarwood lounge chair, exactly the same as the one Gloria occupied. "I missed you at breakfast. *And*, you took the car."

"I had a hair appointment," Gloria said, patting the upturn of the tips of her hair and twisting to present her new do, which had been teased into a bouffant.

"Ah, yes," Rosa said, her voice light with approval of the new style. "It suits you."

"It's blonder," Gloria explained needlessly. "Can you tell? Blond is all the rage!"

"You look fabulous."

Gloria's eyes suddenly flashed with uncertainty. "Do you think so?"

Rosa wasn't sure why Gloria seemed to need so much validation. Then again, with a demanding mother like Aunt Louisa . . .

"Yes, Gloria. You're simply stunning."

"Oh, thank you." Gloria collapsed back into her lounge chair with an expression of relief.

Rosa opened her book, but the words swam

without meaning in front of her. Instead, the sensation of rising into the air on the Ferris wheel captured her thoughts, and how she'd felt both trapped and liberated by the sensation of being suspended in the air. Once she'd let go of the fear of falling—an irrational fear at best since she'd never once heard of a carriage simply falling off such a machine—she'd been captivated by the view. She closed her eyes, and in her mind's eye she could see the ocean off to the west and in the distance, facing east, a range of mountains. Beyond the natural beauty were the sparkling lights, golden white in the town and an explosion of neon in the fairgrounds.

She saw the tops of the heads of people as they moved from ride to ride, or stood in lines to buy cotton candy or paper cartons of buttered popcorn.

Rosa felt the weight of her eyebrows drop as another memory played like a short film; the one featuring Victor Boyd and Don Welks.

Her eyes popped open and she turned her head to stare at Gloria. Her cousin had also let her magazine fall to the patio as she closed her eyes and soaked up the sun.

"Gloria?"

"Uh-huh," Gloria said, sleepily.

"Do you know where Joyce and Don live?"

Gloria opened one eye.

"On Sunnyside Avenue. What do you want to see her for?"

"Not just her," Rosa said, wanting to keep her word

to Miguel and not explain her inquiries away. "I want to see Nancy, and Pauline Van Peridon, sometime too."

Gloria propped up on her elbows, excitement in her eyes. "Are we planning something?"

"Would you like to?"

"Sure. It would be fun." Gloria's expression dropped. "Now that Nancy and Joyce are both married, it's hard to get them out without their husbands. And Nancy's got kids. Marjorie would be up to it. I know Nance was more your friend, but Marjorie is a lot of fun."

"What about Pauline?"

"Oh, yeah. I always forget about her." Gloria's elbows slid back to her side, her eyes closed again as she relaxed on her back. "Marjorie works as a carhop at the Steak and Shake farther down on Cedar Street."

"Steak and what?" Rosa asked.

"Steak and Shake. It's the drive-in restaurant. We should lunch there sometime!"

"Sometime, certainly," Rosa said, thinking suddenly that she would lunch there today, *alone*. Her stomach growled at the thought of food. She swung her legs out, and stood. "It's a little hot for this English flower," she said. "I've not yet adapted to this heat."

"Stay long enough, and you will," Gloria said.

Rosa stared at her cousin, and reluctantly asked her next question. "It's so terrible what happened to Victor Boyd last night, isn't it?"

Gloria's relaxed expression grew tight. She slid her

sunglasses to the tip of her nose and stared up at Rosa. "Ya, of course. I mean, he was a horrible guy, but I certainly didn't wish for him to *actually* die." Pushing her sunglasses back into place she added, "But I can't say I'm broken up about the fact that I never have to worry about running into him again."

12

Now that Gloria had returned with the Bel Air, Rosa was free to take it to run "errands", at least that's what she told Aunt Louisa when she ran into her in the hallway outside Uncle Harold's office where her aunt ran her affairs. She changed into a blue and red summer dress with a matching belt and cloth buttons, and, Gloria would be pleased to know, a full crinoline. Adding a blue half-hat trimmed with a cloth rose, short summer gloves, and red baby doll shoes with heels a little too high to be practical, Rosa took a moment to assess her reflection in the full-length mirror, then added a pearl choker. As her mother was apt to say, one never knew who one would meet and it was good for a lady's confidence to look her best.

Back in the Bel Air, Rosa rounded the corner onto Cedar Street, and a flamingo-pink building came into view. The restaurant section was a large round building with floor-to-ceiling glass windows, which allowed a good view of the cooks making the meals inside. Surrounding the front of the restaurant was a semicircle of parking stalls. She had seen this style of American restaurant on the telly back in London, but she was surprised not only by the vividness of the colors but also to find one so close to her aunt's home. Waitresses wearing pink dresses and white aprons, and quite astonishingly, roller skates, zoomed back and forth between the building and the waiting cars.

Rosa idled the Bel Air just outside the parking stalls and took in her surroundings. It didn't take long to spot Marjorie Davidson—her long red ponytail swinging as she delivered a tray filled with food to a late-forties model Buick. Marjorie looked older than the rest of the carhops, even if the high ponytail gave her a youthful appearance.

The midday sun beat heavily on the Bel Air, so once Rosa was parked, she wound down the passenger window, propped her elbow out, and waited. Marjorie soon rolled out from the building with a menu to greet her.

"Welcome to Steak and Shake," she said, passing Rosa a menu before either recognition hit or she was out of the glare of the sun. "Oh! Rosa! Hi!"

"Hi, Marjorie! Gloria mentioned you worked here, and I had a strong craving for a chocolate milkshake, so here I am." Rosa offered a bright smile. She had often watched her mother put on a disarming smile before launching into a query session.

"The burgers are peachy too," Marjorie said sweetly as if she'd forgotten how put out she'd been on learning of Rosa's association with the police. There didn't seem to be an ounce of offense to her tone now.

"Sounds wonderful," Rosa said. "I'll take one of each."

As Marjorie skated away with her menu and notepad, Rosa rehearsed her plan of questioning. She wanted to get a clear alibi from Marjorie and the other girls without going into details about the murder. Until Gloria's alibi was in place, and Gloria could hear some information on the case, Rosa wanted to be sure it didn't become today's hottest gossip.

The drive-in was a busy place over the lunch hour, and Rosa sang along with The Platters on the radio to pass the time. She often found that distracting oneself could help to unlock a vital clue hidden in the subconscious. When Marjorie finally delivered Rosa's milkshake, she was ready with her first question.

"Listen, Marjorie, would you tell me about that tilt-a-whirl ride? It looked like fun! I've never ridden one, and I was sad to have had Diego with me last night because I wasn't able to join all of you on it."

Marjorie glanced around to survey whether she had a moment to chat. "Oh, it's the boss," she said, excitement in her eyes. "Too bad the line was so long. We all could have gone on it again."

"You were in line for the ride the entire time you left me last night? It was that long?"

As if she felt awful for deserting her, Marjorie placed a hand on Rosa's arm. "If only it had been an outdoor lineup, at least we could have chatted with you while we waited."

"Yes, but you came straight back to find me afterward, right?"

Marjorie nodded. "The tilt-a-whirl exited right near the roller coaster. Not only did we find you right away, but we quickly found out about the, um, incident, with Victor Boyd."

Rosa's next job was to confirm the alibi of Marjorie and her friends. "All of you were in line and on the ride together when it happened, though, correct? All three of you—you, Nancy, and Pauline—would agree on that?"

Marjorie squinted, and Rosa feared she was too on the nose with her question, but then Marjorie held up a finger and said, "Be right back." Rosa sipped her milkshake as she watched her and tried to gauge if Marjorie was avoiding the question.

Zooming toward the round building as if she'd been born wearing roller skates, Marjorie picked up a tray of food, and delivered it to a nearby car, a red two-door Oldsmobile convertible with the black soft-top down. The vehicle, including the bumped nose of the hood, was waxed to a shiny polish with wide chrome fenders sparkling with a mirror finish, and bright white rubber trim on the mag tires. Rosa had both her parents to thank when it came to motor vehicle appreciation.

But it wasn't the car that had gripped Rosa's attention so much as the driver. Henry Van Peridon smiled at Marjorie as if he'd rather have her for lunch than the tall hamburger she'd presented on a plastic tray. Marjorie played with her ponytail and laughed at something Henry said.

A tapping on the hood of the Bel Air made Rosa jump, and she grabbed at her heart. She let out an embarrassed breath when she saw Larry Rayburn's smiling face.

"Pardon me," he said looking sheepish. "I didn't mean to startle ya."

"It's fine," Rosa said. She found herself feeling pleased at this unexpected turn of events. "I'm happy to see you. Do you come here often?"

"More than I should, you could say. I tend to eat on the run." He lifted up a paper bag to prove his point. "Eat at my desk at the morgue. I see ya've discovered American burgers."

Rosa smiled. "That and the milkshakes."

An awkward moment passed between them and Rosa feared Larry might bring up his dinner date offer, which Rosa wasn't quite ready to entertain. She seized the moment to turn the serendipitous meeting to the case.

"Have you had a chance to complete the Victor

Boyd autopsy?" she asked, then added hopefully. "Anything new to report?

Larry shrugged. "Straightforward death by electrocution resulting in cardiac arrest. Heart stopped and never started again." He held up his lunch bag again. "I'm fixin' to eat this while it's still hot. Good to see ya, again, Rosa."

"You too, Larry."

Before Rosa could ponder the significance of this chance meeting, or even determine if anything, indeed, was significant, Marjorie wheeled back over to Rosa.

Rosa's eyebrows jumped in a teasing manner as she tilted her head toward Henry Van Peridon's car. "New fella?"

"Oh, Henry?" Marjorie risked a glance over her shoulder at Henry who hadn't stopped staring at her.

"Ah, I dunno. He's got a nice car and a lot of dough. I know he's shorter than me, but he's decent-looking, doncha think? Works at the Aeronautical Research Center, which means he must be a smart cookie too. I suppose I could do worse."

Rosa supposed that she could. "You were telling me about the tilt-a-whirl ride."

Marjorie blinked like she couldn't understand why Rosa wanted to keep talking about that. "Yeah, the lineup didn't end up being too bad. We were clowning around with Gary, the carnie in charge. Time flew by."

So not only could each of the three friends vouch for each other, Gary the carnie should be able to as well. Rosa would have to pass this new information on to Miguel.

So much for being a *girl on holiday*!

Rosa tried the same tactic with Marjorie as she'd used with Gloria. "What happened with Victor was terrible, wasn't it?"

Marjorie let out a chuckle that Rosa found chilling. "I think there are some people in Santa Bonita that would consider Victor Boyd's accident as an act of fate. As you know, he wasn't exactly frat."

"What?"

"Frat. He wasn't popular. Nobody liked him."

Marjorie pulled away, but Rosa held her arm. "Who in Santa Bonita do you think would want him dead?"

Marjorie's face went through a myriad of expressions as she considered this question. Finally, she came up with, "Gloria's my friend, but I think you should ask her that question."

Rosa blinked back her surprise.

"If she didn't hate Victor Boyd more than anyone in this town, I don't know who did." Marjorie skated away to take her next order, leaving Rosa feeling suddenly chilled.

13

According to the folded map in the glove compartment, Sunnyside Avenue was only a few blocks away. Rosa thought it unlikely that she'd catch Don home from work so early in the afternoon, but Joyce might be around, and Rosa wanted to speak with her alone anyway.

The Welks lived in a middle-unit town house in an area of town that supported those in a lower income bracket, which Rosa found perplexing, since, if memory served her, Joyce's family were rather well-to-do.

Rosa's timing was perfect, as she pulled up to the curb just as Joyce was leaving her home. Dressed in a summer dress with a full skirt, plain pumps, and a silk patterned head scarf tied under her chin, Joyce started down the sidewalk. Her square purse hung by short straps over one forearm, and her hands were covered by cute white gloves that ended at her wrists.

Stepping out of the Bel Air, Rosa called out, "Joyce!"

Joyce turned at the sound of her name, and cupped a gloved hand over her eyes. "Rosa?"

"Yes, hi. I was in the neighborhood, and thought I recognized you."

Joyce's eye narrowed. "What were you doing in *this* neighborhood?" Joyce's gaze landed on the Bel Air, quite easily the most expensive vehicle on the street.

Rosa caught up to Joyce and offered a friendly smile. "Actually, I was looking for you."

"I have an appointment. You can walk to the bus stop with me if you like."

"Or I could drive you," Rosa offered.

"Oh. Okay, that would be nice. I am feeling rather tired."

Joyce relayed the address and short directions as they each opened one of the heavy doors of the Bel Air and slid onto the striped white and yellow leather seats. Joyce ran a finger along the chrome trim of the yellow dash. "Neat chariot!"

Rosa started the engine and pulled out into the wide street. "Thank you. It belongs to my aunt."

"Yeah, you Forresters really suffer."

Rosa ignored the jibe. "How's your family, Joyce?"

"I wouldn't know. They cut me off when I married Don."

"Why would they do that?"

"Because he's poor," Joyce replied, as if the answer were obvious. "He works at a grocery store. My old man wouldn't even consider him worthy of joining the Kilbourne family unless he owned the store. Actually, unless he owned a chain of stores."

Joyce glanced at Rosa with eyes that burned with emotion. "I don't care about money! It doesn't make people happy, I saw that firsthand."

"You must really love Don," Rosa said. She remembered visiting Joyce at the Kilbourne home, a grand house not far from the Forrester mansion.

"I do," Joyce said emphatically. "With all my heart. I don't care that he's poor or *tall*. My dad had a problem with that too. I think Don's handsome, and funny and kind."

Rosa's only impression of Don Welks was what she'd seen of him on the dance floor at the fair, where he seemed very taken with his wife, and then an opposing picture of him fighting with Victor.

"Does Don still work at the grocery store?"

Joyce nodded. "Ralph's on main."

"Were Don and Victor friends?"

"What?" Joyce stared at Rosa as if she were crazy. "He had nothing to do with that nosebleed."

Rosa knew that wasn't true. "So as far as you know, Don had no reason to be upset with Victor Boyd."

"No! I hadn't thought about Victor for ages until Marjorie spotted him at the boardwalk. I don't even think Don knew Victor. What's with all the questions?"

Should Rosa come clean about what she'd seen with Joyce? Her instincts told her to hold on to the information.

"Nothing, I just wondered."

Her comment synchronized with their arrival and Joyce pointed to a commercial building. A list of doctors' names was embossed on the door.

Joyce tilted her head, her eyes twinkling in conspiracy. "I think I'm expecting."

"Oh," Rosa said. "Congratulations."

A smile crossed Joyce's face. "Don doesn't know. I want to surprise him. Please don't tell anyone."

Rosa smiled back. "Your secret is safe with me."

Once Joyce had disappeared into the building, Rosa turned the Bel Air around and headed for Ralph's. She had to be out of *something*.

The enormous sign with the name RALPH'S in red script was visible from the opposite end of the strip. Rosa pulled the Bel Air into one of the angular parking spots in the large attached lot, grabbed her purse, and headed inside.

The supermarket was new to Santa Bonita since the war and this was the first time she'd been in such a large shop. In London, there were myriads of places to shop for one's food and personal needs, but they tended to be smaller and specialize. One shop for bread, another for meat, another for fruit and vegetables. With so much land available per capita in America, businesses could afford to take up more space. Everything a shopper needed could be found under one roof.

A sense of awe settled on Rosa as she wandered down each aisle, every shelf stocked from floor to as high as one could reach with canned and boxed goods. On the perimeter of the store, more produce, dairy, and meat could be found than could possibly feed all the citizens of Santa Bonita.

The abundance of the 1950s was in clear contrast to the scarcity Rosa remembered when she'd lived there in the 1940s.

However, she was not at the market to admire and shop, but to find one very tall employee. She spotted him easily, stocking shelves in the cereal section. He paused when he saw her approach.

"Can I help you find something, ma'am?"

"I'm actually looking for you, Mr. Welks."

His eyes flashed with confusion. "Do I know you?"

"I'm an old friend of Joyce's. Rosa Reed."

"Ah." Don said, resuming his task of removing bags of Quaker Oats oatmeal from a cardboard box and placing them onto the shelf in neat rows. "She did mention you. Back for a visit from England, huh?"

"That's right."

"What'cha want to see me for?"

Rosa decided to get right to the heart of the matter.

"I saw you fighting with Mr. Boyd on the night he was murdered."

Don's long arm stilled, then he removed the last bag of oats from the box, delivered it to its spot, and faced Rosa.

"Hmmm. Joyce told me you were a lady cop in London. Doesn't compute why you're poking at a crime in California."

"I happened to be the one to find the body," Rosa said. "And I work as a consultant with the Santa Bonita police."

Rather a half-truth in this situation, but Rosa left her statement unqualified.

Don let out a long breath through his nose, then checked his watch. "I can take a short break. Can we take this outside in ten minutes?"

"I'll be waiting beside a white and yellow Bel Air."

Rosa used the ten minutes to select a yellow and brown package of peanut M&M's and a bottle of Coca Cola.

A cheerless lady at the cash register announced, "That'll be twenty cents."

Rosa fetched two dimes from her purse and placed them on the counter. One of the first things she'd done after arriving in Santa Bonita was to take the British pound notes she'd brought along and exchange them at the bank for American dollars.

She had eaten half the M&M's when Don Welks,

with his long-legged gait, strolled toward her. Rosa twisted the top of the bag and shoved it into her purse.

"Let's make this quick, okay," Don Welks said without preamble.

"What were you and Mr. Boyd arguing about?"

Don shoved his large fists into the pockets of his pants, the hems uncuffed and barely reaching his ankles.

"I don't see why it matters?"

"It makes you a suspect, Mr. Welks. If you don't talk to me, I can promise you that you'll soon be talking to the police."

Don Welks whipped out one hand and held out his oversized palm. "All right, all right." His shoulders slumped as if he'd lost all his fight and he leaned up against the Bel Air, a transgression Rosa could forgive, especially since it wasn't her vehicle.

"I did something stupid, okay?"

"Was Mr. Boyd blackmailing you?" Rosa stared at the man with compassion. Blackmail was a common motive, and unfortunately made murderers out of perfectly nice people.

Don grabbed the back of his neck, his expression collapsing with a sense of grief. "I shouldn't have married Joyce."

Rosa thought of the reason behind Joyce's doctor's visit. "You don't love her anymore?"

"No, that's not it. I love her too much! But I don't deserve her. I should've listened to her father. He said, *he said*, if I really loved her I should let her go, let her live the life she was born to live."

"What did you do, Mr. Welks? What was Victor Boyd holding over you?"

"I don't have a lot of money, Miss Reed. You can tell that by the kind of job I have. I wanted to do better. I spent two years in community college."

Rosa hoped it wasn't to study anything involving electricity.

"It's where I met Joyce," Don continued. "She was a Kilbourne and didn't need a job to make money. She was there to have fun and meet boys. Unfortunately, she met me."

"And the two of you fell in love."

Don glanced over at Rosa. "Yes. Passionately. And —I take full responsibility for this—she got pregnant."

Rosa hadn't been aware of a child. Don hurried to fill in the blanks.

"Mr. Kilbourne was furious, of course, and immediately made plans for Joyce to be sent away to have the baby, give it up, and come back to her life here like nothing had happened. That, and I had to promise to leave town. Joyce doesn't know this, but he offered me five thousand dollars to step out of her life.

"But Joyce would have none of that idea. She insisted that we marry. How could I say no? I loved her and she was carrying my child.

"Mr. Kilbourne is the kind of man who is used to getting his own way. He told Joyce if she went through with the wedding, she'd be cut off from the Kilbourne fortune, her and the baby."

Don pinched his eyes shut as he finished the story. "We got married, spent three days at Long Beach on our honeymoon. Two weeks later, Joyce lost the baby."

"I'm so sorry," Rosa said sincerely. She waited, hoping Don would get back to her original question and finally answer it. She was rewarded.

"One day at the store, a customer dropped his wallet. He'd taken off his jacket and it had fallen out of the pocket without him noticing. Next thing I know, the wallet's sitting on the floor and the man's disappeared around the corner. I immediately picked it up, and I meant to give it back right away, but when I had it in my hands—well, we were short on rent that month. Instead of running after the man, I dropped it into my apron."

"And Victor Boyd saw this?"

Don nodded heavily. "I'd taken the cash out of the wallet and mailed the wallet back to the address on the owner's driver's license. A week later, Victor Boyd stops me in this parking lot and asks me what I did with the wallet. I tried to deny any wrong, but Victor knew what I did; any accusation, true or false, would ruin my reputation and get me fired. Worse, he threatened to tell Joyce."

Don checked his watch then pushed away from the Bel Air. "You officially know more about me than my wife, Miss Reed."

As he started to walk away, Rosa called, "Mr. Welks, the course you were taking in college, did it happen to be electrical engineering?"

Don Welks slowly nodded. "Yes, Miss Reed. But I didn't kill Victor Boyd."

14

The funfair was once again open for business, and Rosa made an impromptu stop. Strolling along the boardwalk, she noted that the place was busy though the ambiance was relaxed. People took turns on the rides, which had shorter lines than in the evening. It was obvious by their casual attire, that some fairgoers had strolled in from the beach when in the mood for cotton candy. In the background, ongoing carnival music played, interrupted occasionally by carnies calling, "Step right up!" All the fanfare blended into an air of muted excitement.

Her initial search for Mr. Henderson appeared futile, when all she found at the fairground's office was a lopsided sign hanging from the door handle that read, "Back in 30 Minutes".

Rosa returned to the roller coaster, which was still surrounded by rope, and several "Closed for Maintenance" signs. People approached the roller coaster and let out moans of disappointment.

From there, Rosa made her way to The Flying Machine—the ride Jimmy had operated the night before, when Victor died. She was happy to see this ride was operational, even if it wasn't Jimmy at the controls this time. Instead, a lean man in his mid-thirties was busy letting a new batch of little riders onto the small planes. She called to him as soon as his ride was up and running.

"Have you seen Mr. Henderson, the fair manager?"

"Huh?" The attendant turned to face Rosa. His dark hair was unruly, and he wore a few days' worth of scruff on his chin. "Uh, yeah. Maybe ten minutes ago. He came by here with a cop interviewing all the carnies who worked yesterday."

Rosa's heart skipped a beat at the thought of Miguel somewhere nearby. "Any idea which way they went?"

"Don't know. Maybe the Ferris wheel." The man returned to his controls.

Rosa hesitated. Did she risk being seen by Miguel? He'd been rather clear that he no longer needed nor wanted her on this case. If he found out she was still nosing about in what was clearly not her business, he might—what? What was the worst that could happen? He'd threaten to not talk to her? Not share clues?

She was about to step in with a mom and her

young son carrying a red balloon, passing in front of her, as awkward as that might have been, when Miguel seemed to materialize out of nowhere. He inexplicably looked in her direction and caught her eye.

His eyes narrowed as she lifted her hand halfway and weakly wiggled her fingers.

"Rosa!" Miguel called out, his expression returning to neutral. Mr. Henderson, walking with him, grimaced further at seeing her.

Once the distance between them closed, Miguel said, "Should I ask why you're here?"

"Uh, I actually had a hankering for some cotton candy."

Miguel's lips twitched. "*Hankering*? Have you been to see Dr. Rayburn?"

Rosa blushed at being caught out at using a term more common in the south, but before she could protest, Mr. Henderson loudly grumbled, "I gotta get back to work."

Miguel remained diplomatic. "Thank you for your help this morning, Mr. Henderson. I appreciate it."

Mr. Henderson didn't acknowledge the gratitude and instead strode toward his office. Rosa held her childish urge to stick out her tongue at the rude man and closed the gap between herself and Miguel.

She dared to ask, "What did you find out this morning?"

Miguel paused, and for a moment Rosa thought he

wasn't going to say, but then he said, "I've cleared Mr. Henderson from our list of suspects."

Rosa raised an eyebrow. "How so? The man had motive and certainly the means to do it."

"Mr. Henderson doesn't much care for any of his employees and says he had no reason to pick on Victor Boyd in particular. He thinks they're all a lazy bunch of ne'er-do-wells and would love to hire just one guy who didn't try to clock out early or clock in late, or swipe extra change from a customer."

"But if you'll recall," Rosa pressed, "Mr. Thompson said Mr. Henderson was afraid of Mr. Boyd."

Miguel lifted a shoulder. "It's a case of 'he said, he said'. No evidence to support it. And even if the manager had reason to fear Victor Boyd, it doesn't mean he killed him."

"It doesn't mean he didn't," Rosa returned, feeling the heat of stubbornness spreading across her chest. "He had means, motive, and opportunity."

"When I interviewed Mr. Henderson, he said Victor had taken charge of his ride and didn't put up with troublemaking patrons," Miguel said. "It was a necessary quality for someone operating the roller coaster. If Mr. Henderson had been ready to fire anyone, he said it would have been Jimmy, who was always letting kids ride who were smaller than the height requirement or other things that Mr. Henderson felt put his fair at risk."

This meant that Jimmy Thompson had stretched the truth to his favor, which wasn't at all surprising. Rosa had learned it was human nature to do so, especially when one felt threatened.

Miguel gave Rosa a meaningful look. "Mr. Henderson says he's not going to let Jimmy go until everything has settled down with the investigation—but he will fire him, eventually."

"This doesn't completely clear Mr. Henderson," Rosa said.

Miguel conceded with another shrug.

They arrived at the roller coaster, and Miguel stopped just outside the rope. "Actually, I don't think Mr. Henderson had the means to do it."

Rosa wrinkled her forehead at this. Miguel lifted the rope for her to duck under, and he followed her to the other side.

After opening the gate to the control platform, he instructed Rosa, "Go on. Step up."

Rosa hesitated. Someone had died of electrocution in this very spot last night, after all. But she trusted Miguel and his electrician that all had been restored to working order. She stepped up and then turned to him in question.

"Now, bend down as though you're going to remove the lower panel like my electrician did earlier."

Smoothing the back of her skirt tightly to avoid flashing Miguel, something she'd rather not, she followed his instructions. Miguel, ever the gentleman, stepped back so his line of sight didn't inadvertently line up.

"Okay," she said. "What now?"

"Picture Mr. Henderson trying to accomplish the position you're in now. Or actually, don't bother picturing it, because it couldn't happen. When I asked him to do the same thing, he didn't fit. There's no way he could have squeezed himself into the bottom half of the control platform to manipulate the electrical wires—especially with the gate closed, which he'd need to have done or else someone would've seen him."

Rosa's mind flashed to the Steak and Shake restaurant. "One too many hamburgers and milkshakes?"

She was rewarded with a single dimple.

"When I asked Mr. Henderson to get in that position, he got a cramp in his leg so painful he had to lie on a bench for ten minutes. He couldn't have done it without help nor in the short time he would have had while Victor had stepped away."

If Mr. Henderson couldn't fit for being too rotund, Don Welks' height would likely create the same obstacle.

"I've also cleared the carnie named Skip Stevens. He was taking tickets on the roller coaster, and the patrons loading the cars had a clear view of him. He connected me with two of them just during the time we were talking today. Finding a dead body shook up the kid. He said it took everything he had to come to work this morning. He didn't want anything to do with the rides and asked Mr. Henderson if he could sell popcorn."

Rosa stepped down from the platform, mentally checking Mr. Henderson, Don Welks, and Skip Stevens from her list of suspects.

"Where's Deputy Diego?" Miguel asked once they were both outside the yellow rope again.

"I'm afraid I had to relieve him of his badge, due to his earlier bout of bad behavior."

Miguel nodded with a smirk. "I see. Do you plan on reinstating him?"

"Probably. It was only his first offence."

"Good, because I'm not sure we can solve this case without him."

Rosa let the word *we* ring in her head for a moment before adding, "I'll let him know you said that."

"You don't think it will go to his head?"

Miguel and his dimples were trying to lighten things up, but Rosa could only think about how they'd circled back to square one.

15

Rosa wrinkled her nose. "You're back to looking for a needle in the haystack of a thousand people who visited the boardwalk last night?"

"Not necessarily," Miguel said. "Mr. Henderson mentioned a carnie who's working this afternoon that was here yesterday. A Gary McCooey," he said, motioning his chin towards a huge building. "He runs the tilt-a-whirl."

As they headed to the ride, Rosa explained how Marjorie had mentioned Gary. "Hopefully we can get my friends off the suspect list," she said.

"Agreed. I feel like I'm getting different stories from the workers about the animosity between employees. I'm interested to hear what Mr. McCooey says about how Victor got on with his colleagues." He glanced down at Rosa. "You went to school with the guy. What's your take on why everyone hated Victor Boyd so much?"

Rosa thought back to that hazy time in her life. "I don't think he was always the mean bully everyone remembers now," Rosa replied. "I have vague memories of Victor with a genuine smile on his face and having fun with the rest of the students. But that was wartime and situations could change in an instant."

Miguel added quietly, "And people."

Rosa's throat almost closed out at the implication. *She* had changed. They *both* had changed.

"Um, yes," she managed to mutter. Pressing on, she continued, "Several students I knew during those days had lost parents or loved ones as a result of the fighting. There were times when it felt like every day at school someone would be sobbing at their desk, or their desk would simply be empty. But with Victor, it was different. After his dad was killed, he turned into a terror overnight. It was as though Victor blamed the other students for his father's death."

"His father died?" Miguel asked as they neared the tilt-a-whirl building. "You're sure about that?"

"Yes. Why? The accident made front-page headlines."

Miguel shook his head. "It's just . . . when I broke the news to Victor's parents, they mentioned that they hadn't heard from their son in years. They showed me a family photo of when Victor was a small child standing next to his younger sister. I'm pretty sure the father in the photograph was the same man I spoke to."

"Could he have been his stepdad?" Rosa asked. "Perhaps the two men looked alike."

"They both go by the name Boyd. Sanchez would've found out by now if they weren't related."

After entering the unlit building that housed the tilt-a-whirl, Miguel and Rosa paused, their eyes adjusting to the darkness that was in juxtaposition with the flashing neon lights. The carnie Rosa assumed was Mr. McCooey had just loaded a new batch of riders. Several seashell-shaped cars spun in circles on their tracks, all the while weaving around one another in a way that evoked fear, or at the very least, adrenaline, in Rosa's veins, especially as they gained speed. However, she thought with a slight smile, a trip on a carnival ride wasn't much different from driving through London with her mother at the wheel. Rosa's experience with Gloria's driving wasn't much better.

Mr. McCooey's eyes darted in several directions when he saw them approach the platform.

"Police?" he said.

Rosa clucked her tongue. Some people had a sixth sense when it came to the law.

"It's okay, Mr. McCooey," Miguel said, "I'm Detective Belmonte from the Santa Bonita Police Department, and this is WPC Reed from the London Metropolitan Police."

Mr. McCooey's eyes narrowed. "What's going on that we need international police involved?"

"I'm simply consulting," Rosa said smoothly, then asked, "Did you hear anything about what happened to Victor Boyd last night?"

Mr. McCooey let out a low whistle, and for the first time, Rosa noticed the large gap between his teeth. With hair greased and combed into a sloppy fringe—the fashionable duckbill—he crossed large biceps across his chest, his T-shirt untucking from one side of his work jeans, which tapered to narrow cuffs at his ankles.

"Yeah, everyone's talking about it," Mr. McCooey said. "Someone knocked him off?"

"Who's everyone?" Miguel asked.

"All the carnies. We talk. Anything happens 'round here, we all know about it."

"How well did you know Victor Boyd?" Rosa asked.

"As much as I know anyone at this place. He did his job; I did mine. A bunch of us went for a beer after closing sometimes, but can't say I ever had a conversation with the guy."

"So, you two were on friendly terms?" Miguel confirmed.

Another gap-toothed whistle. "I guess. Same as anyone."

"Same as Jimmy Thompson or Skip Stevens?" Those were the only other carnies Rosa knew by name.

"Ha!" Mr. McCooey sneered. "Skip, sure, but that little twerp Jimmy? Nope, he ain't like the rest of us."

Rosa shared a look with Miguel. More than a little animosity there, aimed at someone other than their victim.

"Mr. Thompson and Victor Boyd were friends, though, right?"

Now Mr. McCooey's laugh came with raised eyebrows. "Friends? No way. Victor hated that runt. Poked fun at him all the time." Mr. McCooey smacked a palm with his fist. "Said he'd give him a knuckle sandwich."

Rosa grimaced. *That* sounded *exactly* like the Victor Boyd she'd known at the end of her schooling in Santa Bonita. Before they could ask further questions, Mr. McCooey stopped the ride and let on a new set of riders. As he did so, Miguel and Rosa conversed in hushed tones.

"Perhaps you shouldn't have released Jimmy Thompson quite so fast," Rosa said.

Miguel gave his head a quick shake. "We had nothing to keep him on, but I'd say we certainly need to speak to him again."

"For a third time," Rosa pointed out. If anyone seemed guilty, it was Jimmy Thompson. He'd admitted to being on Victor's control platform and rigging the bucket yesterday. Who was to say he hadn't removed the rubber sheath and moved a wire simultaneously?

Gary McCooey returned.

Without any preamble, Miguel asked, "Any other carnies that Mr. Boyd didn't like? Or who didn't like him?"

"Nah," Mr. McCooey said. "We all joked. All got along. It's Jimmy Thompson that never fit in. I'm surprised he's not the dead one."

Miguel glanced at Rosa, but she had another question at the ready. "There were three ladies who came through your ride around the time of the incident."

Gary chuckled, relaxing as though he, too, knew this interview was nearly over. "Lotsa ladies were on my ride yesterday," he said. "You want me to remember three of 'em?"

Yes, Rosa *did* want that. Undeterred, she described the dresses her new friends had been wearing. After mentioning Marjorie's long red ponytail and striking green A-line dress covered with black polka-dots, his eyes noticeably brightened.

He snapped his fingers. "Her, I remember. The redhead! She was flirting with me!"

Rosa could imagine the wild-hearted Marjorie flirting with this carnie but not with any serious intention. "And she was with some other ladies?"

"Yeah, yeah. I think there were two of 'em. Talked to me the whole time they wove back and forth in that line," he said, pointing. Rosa looked to the roped area that guided riders through the building. It would have taken the ladies a good hour to get through the line last night, which well accounted for their whereabouts during the time of Victor's death.

"And the lineup was full yesterday afternoon?" Rosa confirmed, motioning to the queue.

"Sure was. Least three times as many as this."

Rosa looked to Miguel, and in silent agreement, they nodded and turned back to Mr. McCooey. Thanking him in unison, they made their way out through the exit.

They squinted as the bright light of day greeted them, and Rosa cupped a hand over her eyes against the glare of the afternoon sun.

"Looks like you can cross your friends off our list," Miguel said. "Well, except for Gloria, but I'm about to head to the Lobster Bar to confirm her alibi."

Rosa was a little surprised Miguel hadn't already done so, but on the other hand, his delay spoke to its lack of priority and that Gloria wasn't considered a serious contender.

"Where are you going next?" Miguel asked.

Rosa had a destination in mind, but she wasn't about to tell Miguel.

"I'm going home," she said. It wasn't a lie so much as a tad misleading. She was going to go home *eventually*.

16

Rosa parked across the street from the Santa Bonita Library, willing her pulse to calm down. Pulling a handkerchief from her purse, she pressed its cool surface against her forehead. She was perspiring because she was yet unused to the persistent California heat. It had nothing to do with that building.

Whatsoever.

Closing her eyes, Rosa inhaled deeply through her nose and slowly released it through her mouth. She was being silly. She'd already been in Miguel's company far more than she'd dreamed since her arrival in Santa Bonita. How hard would it be to face the ghosts of the past?

Hard.

But, Rosa told herself, she was stronger than she thought, and after the first few minutes inside, once the onslaught of the memories was over, she could put it all behind her. She glanced at the empty seat beside her, wishing she had her furry deputy to talk to. Diego would purr appropriately and encourage her to get on with it.

It's just an ordinary library, nothing more nor less.

Rosa rallied her reserves of strength and opened the driver's door of the Bel Air. Just one step at a time was all it took.

Suddenly she was in her school outfit, a slender skirt that landed mid-calf with a kick pleat at the back, a white blouse, and a scarf tied in a bow at her neck. Her hair was longer, with the side pieces pinned up into curls on the top of her head and the back smoothly curled under.

Like now, Rosa's heart beat as strongly then, because in those days visits to the library no longer meant studying for exams, but clandestinely meeting up with Miguel.

Pulling on the brass handle of the heavy wooden door, Rosa stepped inside and was immediately accosted by the comforting smell of books. The Santa Bonita Library wasn't large, and reminded Rosa more of a large West Coast house that had all the utilities and walls stripped out of it, and couldn't compare to the vast and ancient British Library. But it serviced the small community well and due to the community college, also had a good collection of non-fiction trade books.

Inside, nothing had changed. The shelves were situated exactly the same way as a decade before, with the same tables in the same places. Even the librarian, Miss Cumberbatch, a slender lady who, except for shorter hair and a few more lines on her face, seemed unchanged.

Her serious expression took on a look of surprise when she spotted Rosa. With a husky, low voice imitating a whisper she said, "Miss Reed?"

Rosa took quick strides to the checkout desk, and keeping her voice low, replied, "Hello, Miss Cumberbatch. Is it still Miss Cumberbatch?"

The side of the librarian's mouth twitched. "It is. I suppose you've got a new name, though."

"Actually not. I've not yet married."

Miss Cumberbatch's eyes shone with something akin to camaraderie. "What brings you back to Santa Bonita?"

"My family. I thought it was time for a visit."

"Of course. You are part of the Forrester clan."

"That's right."

"Can I help you with something? Or are you here to browse."

"I'm here to browse, thank you."

Rosa knew this library like the back of her hand, and knew exactly where she wanted to go.

And where she didn't. Specifically, the area behind the lesser-visited section of the ancient history tomes. Even turning her back to that corner couldn't keep the memories flooding in. The very first time Miguel had spoken to her, and how enamored she felt to be found of interest by an American soldier. Miguel almost always wore his uniform in those days, with a service hat on a closely shaved head.

She'd been undone by his smile, and those dimples! Rosa was amazed her weakened knees were capable of holding her up at all.

She'd lacked the wisdom that comes with age and hard knocks, and had steadfastly ignored all the warning signs that clearly yelled that their young romance was doomed, and that she'd suffer for far longer than the short amount of joyous time she'd so readily signed up for.

Shaking off the reverie with a violent shudder, Rosa went to a section on the opposite side of the library, to the shelf where books about the topic of electricity and electrical engineering could be found.

Running her fingers along the spines, Rosa removed a textbook of interest and opened the cover to the page that held all the copyright information. On the flyleaf, a pocket added by the librarians held the sign-out card. Each borrower's name was written on the card, along with a notation of the date it was due back to the library, the most recent borrower listed at the bottom.

Rosa's heart stopped. The last person to check out the textbook was Gloria Forrester!

Rosa quickly removed another manual, and then a

third, and her horror built. Gloria's name occurred in each one.

What on earth was Gloria doing with these textbooks? Surely she had no interest in the science of electricity? At least not beyond the scope of one book.

"Rosa?"

Rosa startled at the sound of her name. More accurately at the *voice* which spoke her name.

The textbook in her hand slipped to the floor.

"Miguel? I thought you were headed to the Lobster Bar?"

"I thought you were going home."

"I am. I just thought I'd stop in the library first." A nervous laugh followed. "You know how I like to read."

Miguel picked up the textbook and gave her a knowing look. "It seems great minds think alike."

Which explained why Miguel was in the same section. They both wanted to educate themselves on the mechanics of the crime that had resulted in Victor Boyd's death.

Rosa selected the two books still on the shelf. "Well, I think these will do."

"You know that you're not officially on this case, right? Your aunt hasn't swayed the mayor to bring you on board this time."

Rosa held the books tightly to her chest. "I know. I'm just curious by nature."

"Curiosity killed the cat."

"Don't bring Diego into this. He doesn't even know I'm here."

Miguel's lips twitched, before forming a full smile, dimples and all. "At least leave a book for me."

Rosa nodded her chin to the one still in his hand. "That's the best one, anyway."

The aisle between the shelving was barely wide enough for two people to pass through, especially with the swing skirt she wore and the full crinoline! Rosa vowed to wear slender pencil dresses from now on.

She took a step to bypass Miguel. He did the same, forcing them to step into each other, closing the distance between their faces. Miguel's copper eyes reflected brightly in the lamplight.

Rosa swallowed and took another sidestep, but Miguel instinctively did the same. They were trapped in an awkward dance!

"Excuse me," Rosa muttered. She waited until Miguel had stepped aside, then brushed past. If she'd hoped he'd stay put, or continue in the other direction, she was to be disappointed. Miguel stepped out of the aisle right behind her.

Rosa's eyes landed on the obscure door at the rear of the building. A glance at Miguel confirmed that he was doing the same. That door led to the community park, to the place where they had had their first kiss, and where they had said their heart-wrenching goodbyes.

Oh dear.

She had to get out of there.

Rosa hurried to the checkout desk, keeping her eyes on Miss Cumberbatch, who performed her duties perfunctorily, completely oblivious to Rosa's distress. When the last book had been date stamped, Rosa practically ran out of the library, leaving without another word to Miguel.

Her feelings for Miguel couldn't be more obvious than if she raised them up a flagpole on a windy day.

17

As with the rest of the mansion, the dining room was well outfitted with modern furniture—a long, sleek Danish table built for eight filled the center of the room and a matching buffet and hutch lined a peach-colored wall. Looking rather spritely in a yellow and blue floral dress, Grandma Sally sat at the table along with Aunt Louisa, Gloria, and Clarence.

Rosa, having waited in the driveway until she had full emotional composure, headed for the table with a smile on her face. "Hi, everyone."

Señora Gomez carried a large platter of roasted chicken into the dining room and set it in the center of the table.

"Señora Gomez," Rosa said cheerily. "Smells delectable!"

Rosa claimed a seat nearest Clarence, nodded

subtly, and then turned to her aunt. "Aunt Louisa, how was your day?"

"Good enough. Nothing new to report."

"I, for one, had a fabulous day," Gloria said, helping herself to a bowl filled with mashed potatoes. "I got a new hairdo." She patted her blonde locks. "Excluding Rosa, I can't believe none of the rest of you noticed!"

"I noticed, dear," Aunt Louisa said dryly. "It makes you look older."

Rosa wasn't sure if her aunt meant it as a criticism, but Gloria didn't take it that way.

"I look more mature, don't I?" she said. "I want to be taken more seriously."

Clarence snorted into his fist.

"Clarence!" Gloria protested, then appealed to Aunt Louisa. "Mother?"

"Clarence, the wise know when to keep their thoughts to themselves."

Grandma Sally muttered, "Which is exactly why I'm not saying anything."

Gloria's distress leaned toward the volcanic, and Rosa hurried to ward off an emotional explosion. "As I said earlier, Gloria, I think you look lovely. It's only a tad difficult to get used to your new look, but you'll most certainly be the envy of your friends."

"Oh, thank you, Rosa," Gloria said before turning on her family. "See, why can't you all be a bit more encouraging?"

"I am encouraging," Clarence said. "I had a tickle in my nose and you mistook my intention."

As Rosa passed the salad and potatoes around, Gloria asked, "So how is your investigation going?"

It was a benign question, and coming from anyone else, Rosa's heart wouldn't have skipped a beat, but she couldn't forget about the library books signed out by Gloria.

"I wouldn't know," Rosa said. "It's not really my investigation."

"I think they should shut that monstrosity down and send it on its way," Grandma Sally said. "I don't like the crowds."

Aunt Louisa's fork paused midair. "Mother, when was the last time you went to town, much less to the boardwalk?"

"Maybe I'd go more if my only daughter would take me."

Aunt Louisa's eyes darted to Rosa, who immediately felt the stab of her step-grandmother's faux pas. Rosa's mother, Ginger, had been a child of eight when Sally Hartigan married her father, George. Rosa knew the story about how her maternal grandmother had died shortly after her mother was born, and that Sally was the only mother Ginger Reed had ever known.

Grandma Sally's watery eyes registered how she'd misspoken. "You know what I mean. I love Ginger, but she doesn't live here, does she? She can't very well drive me around."

"I can take you out," Rosa offered.

Grandma Sally let out a quick, short breath. "It seems to me that you are fairly busy doing whatever it is you do when you're gone. You're hardly home."

Rosa felt the sting of her step-grandmother's chastisement. The elderly lady was lonely, and Rosa determined to carve out time to spend watching television with Grandma Sally the next time her favorite shows were on. She cast a glance at Clarence, a renewed sense of respect filling her, as she realized, whether her cousin sincerely enjoyed the daytime soap operas or not, he spent the time with his grandmother.

The conversation turned to the weather, which was a rather mundane topic in this part of the world. Fortunately, the doorbell rang and interrupted the bland interaction.

"Who on earth can that be?" Grandma Sally said with a hand to her chest. Times of surprise often brought out the strength of her Bostonian accent. Her wrinkled lips tightened, and she sent Aunt Louisa a look of accusation. "Did you make a social engagement for this evening without informing me again?"

Aunt Louisa looked scandalized. "I did not."

Bledsoe, the butler, entered ready to announce who'd had the nerve to come to the Forrester mansion uninvited.

"Bledsoe?" Aunt Louisa said. "Spit it out. Who's at the door?"

"Detective Belmonte, ma'am." His eyes darted to Rosa. "For Miss Reed."

Rosa felt all her blood pool in her knees. After their encounter at the library, Rosa had hoped for at least a full day to recover. She patted her mouth with a cloth napkin, then pushed away from the table. "Excuse me, please."

Not above a touch of vanity, Rosa peered into the mirror hanging in the hall. She patted her chestnut hair and, having a tube of lipstick tucked in her dress pocket, quickly applied a fresh coat of cherry red to her lips—smacking them with a sense of satisfaction.

She found Miguel and Detective Sanchez waiting, hats in hands. Miguel's expression was serious. Definitely *not* a social call.

"Miguel?" Rosa said, feeling a sense of dread. "What's wrong?"

"I'm afraid we're here to fetch your cousin. I wanted to give you the courtesy of a warning."

Oh dear. Everything Rosa had been fearing was coming to pass.

"Gloria?"

"I'm afraid we have to ask Miss Gloria Forrester to accompany us to the police station for questioning concerning the murder of Victor Boyd."

Rosa held in a nervous chuckle. "You can't be serious."

Marjorie's suggestion that Gloria had hated Victor

Boyd more than anyone came back to Rosa now, and her stomach dropped from within her.

"What about the Lobster Bar?" Rosa had hoped Gloria's alibi was a sure thing, but Miguel answered with one slow shake of his head.

Gloria stepped into the fray. "Rosa? Is everything all right?"

Before Rosa could relay the bad news, Aunt Louisa, Clarence, and Grandma Sally had filed into the foyer. Rosa let out a frustrated breath. The Forrester family members were drawn to drama like rowers to the River Thames.

Miguel repeated his request. "We're here to ask Miss Gloria Forrester to accompany us to the station for questioning."

"How ridiculous!" Grandma Sally sputtered.

Aunt Louisa eyed Miguel with eyes of fire. "You've always been trouble, Mr. Belmonte."

"Aunt Louisa?" Rosa felt faint with humiliation. Aunt Louisa wasn't going to bring *that* up, was she? Not now.

Aunt Louisa turned her disdain on Rosa. "I don't know what you ever saw in him, and now that you've come back, he's determined to shame our family name once again."

"Aunt Louisa!"

Rosa dared a glimpse at Miguel. His eyes, ordinarily warm pools of coppery brown, were dark and determined, his mouth a hard, straight line. He breathed hard through his nose before meeting Rosa's eyes.

"I'm sorry, Rosa." Then to Gloria, "Miss Forrester, please come with us."

Gloria swallowed, her eyes glassing over with fear.

Rosa took her hand. "It's going to be okay. I'll be right behind you."

"I'll have your badge, young man," Aunt Louisa snapped, as Gloria stepped in between Miguel and Detective Sanchez. Then almost as an afterthought she added, "We have the best lawyers, Gloria. Don't worry!"

18

In front of the police station, Rosa brought the Bel Air to a skidding stop right behind Miguel's police cruiser and jumped out. Detective Sanchez opened the back door of the cruiser and assisted Gloria as she stepped out of it.

Gloria's eyes watered when she saw Rosa was already there. "Oh, Rosa! I don't know what's happening."

"It's all right," Rosa said, feeling not at all like things were all right. "I'm sure it's just a misunderstanding."

Miguel flashed her a warning look. "I'm afraid you'll have to refrain from speaking for the time being."

Rosa protested, "Miguel!"

"It's not personal," Miguel said gently. "Delvecchio is a stickler for protocol, and in this situation, I have to agree."

Rosa begrudgingly admitted to the wisdom of that. Otherwise, Aunt Louisa might have a leg to stand on, Miguel could lose his job, and worse, things could go terribly wrong for Gloria. Rosa hadn't felt this miserable since the moment, halfway down the aisle in St. George's Church in London, when she was struck with a moment of clarity and knew she couldn't go through with her nuptials.

Gloria repeatedly looked over her shoulder at Rosa as they made their way inside and through the precinct. Rosa tried to keep her face from showing panic and simply offered her cousin a smile and a nod each time she looked back. Miguel guided Gloria into an interrogation room, the same one Rosa had sat in with Jimmy Thompson less than twelve hours before.

Miguel held up a palm and shook his head. "You know you can't join in on this one, right?"

"Of course, I know. Just, you'll have to wait for her lawyer, won't you?"

"I'm certain one is on the way."

"Yes, right, but—"

Miguel stepped close and spoke into Rosa's ear. "You can watch through the mirror. Just don't draw attention to yourself." He walked away without looking back at her, and Rosa felt immense gratitude.

Confirming that the coast was clear, Rosa eased open the door to the room on the other side of the one-way mirror and slipped inside. She watched as Miguel offered Gloria a half-smile. A second later, a wooden speaker mounted on the wall crackled to life and through it, she heard him ask, "Can I get you coffee or water?"

Gloria, sitting stiffly in one of the hard wooden chairs, nodded. "Water."

Miguel gave Detective Sanchez a quick nod, and the officer left on what Rosa presumed was a run for water. She tapped on the mirror.

Both Miguel and Gloria turned toward the sound, Gloria looking perplexed and Miguel looking cross. As she hoped, Miguel excused himself and joined her behind the mirror.

"Rosa?"

"I just need to know what happened at the Lobster Bar. Her alibi didn't check out, did it?"

Miguel suddenly looked very tired. Rosa thought he was about to dismiss her, but then he said, "The manager of the Surfside Lobster Bar, a Mr. Richard Hollick, is well acquainted with the Forrester family. He knew Clarence by name, and Gloria, Louisa, and even Louisa's late husband, Harold."

"And?"

"Richard Hollick claimed he hadn't seen Gloria Forrester in at least a year."

Rosa opened her mouth, but before she could ask, Miguel answered her next question.

"I also interviewed three of the waitresses who claimed to know Gloria Forrester. They didn't see her last night. Have you been to the restaurant?"

Rosa shook her head. "No."

"It's not a big place. Gloria couldn't have used their restroom facilities without someone seeing her. In fact, we must assume, since they are confirmed acquaintances, that Gloria would've extended a greeting to someone. At any rate, without a witness that can place Gloria at the Lobster Bar during that time, she doesn't have an alibi."

"That doesn't mean she killed Victor Boyd."

"No, but her lying about her whereabouts demands further investigation. I was able to connect with your friend Joyce Welks through Detective Sanchez's contacts, and she insisted that Gloria had an intense hatred for Victor Boyd. Do you know about her history with Boyd? Or her feelings toward him?"

"Everyone in school hated Victor Boyd," Rosa murmured as if this information would somehow make up for the fact that her cousin had blatantly lied. "But she was a lot younger than him. For all I know, she didn't have reason to know him at all."

"Speaking of Victor Boyd," Miguel said. "Sanchez looked into the census for the Boyd family. Turns out that Victor's father, Joseph Boyd, wasn't killed in the war. He was, in fact, the man I'd interviewed, alive and well. Sanchez spoke to him in person and confirmed it."

Rosa ducked her chin in confusion. "I don't understand. Why would Victor have lied about such a thing?

If he was that desperate to fit in or to feel people's compassion, wouldn't he have been nicer to everyone?"

Rosa was processing out loud, but Miguel answered her anyway.

"His dad's so-called death was a cover-up for where he really went." Miguel rubbed the back of his neck. "Mr. Joseph Boyd was imprisoned in December 1941 on charges of draft evasion and participation in a draft-card burning."

Somehow Victor Boyd's extreme badgering of several of the other students at school now made sense. While other parents were dying with honor in the war or helping the war effort, Victor's father had been dishonored. Victor had lied so that no one would discover the real reason his father was out of the picture.

Miguel mouthed, "I'm sorry," before backing out the room, and Rosa was once again alone behind the one-way mirror.

Miguel stepped back into the interrogation room just as Gloria's lawyer arrived. The man, dressed in his brown suit with gray hair trimmed short, looked vaguely familiar. Rosa assumed she had met him at some point during her younger years when she'd been in Aunt Louisa's company.

After delivering the glass of water to Gloria, Detective Sanchez sat opposite the lawyer and set up the reel-to-reel recording equipment. Miguel took the remaining chair.

Gloria's eyes were glossy with apprehension, and Rosa felt immense sympathy. She knew what it was like to be in her cousin's position. As Vivien Eveleigh's best friend, Rosa had automatically been put on the suspects' list for her murder, and even though she was soon cleared, the experience of being questioned as if she could be capable of murder had shaken her.

"I'm assuming you've refrained from asking my client any questions until I arrived?" the lawyer said.

"Of course, Mr. Nabor," Miguel replied. "But now that we are all here, let's begin."

Detective Sanchez turned on the recording equipment. After stating the location of the station, the date, and the room number, he gave the names of those in attendance.

Miguel cleared his throat. "Miss Forrester, we'd like to ask you a few questions regarding the death of Victor Boyd."

"I didn't kill him," Gloria blurted.

Mr. Nabor raised a hand in warning. "Miss Forrester, I must remind you that you're not required to answer."

"I want to get this straightened out." She splayed open her hands. "I didn't kill Victor, and I don't know who did."

Miguel appeared unfazed by Gloria's outbursts. "What were your feelings toward Mr. Boyd?"

Rosa pinched her lips. She wished Miguel wouldn't bring up hearsay, but she knew it would come up in court anyway, should it get to that. Better to get to the root of the matter now, but still, it rankled Rosa to watch it.

"I didn't care for him," Gloria answered, "but I didn't think he should die. More like go to jail."

"How did you know this boy who was so much older than you in school?" Miguel asked.

Rosa wondered the same thing.

Gloria glanced at Mr. Nabor, who repeated, "You don't have to answer anything you don't want to."

Rosa silently urged Gloria to speak freely and honestly. Quieting herself now would only make her appear guilty.

Gloria placed her hands flat on the table and looked down at them. "When I was eleven, I had an . . . encounter with Victor at school."

"An encounter?" Miguel pressed. "Do you mean he attacked you?"

"Oh Lord!" Rosa's hands flew to her mouth. How had she never known this?

But Gloria explained. "Not attacked, exactly. He ripped a gold pendant from my neck. It had been a gift from my dad before he went off to war and was my most prized possession. At the time, we hadn't heard from Daddy for several months, and in fact, we didn't hear from him ever again, so the loss of the pendant was heartbreaking to me. Victor said if I told anyone, he'd find me and make sure I never talked about anything again. I ended up lying to my mother; I told her I'd lost it. She was so upset, calling me careless and irresponsible."

Rosa felt a wave of pity for Gloria.

Gloria finished her account by saying, "It took me years before I could even speak about Victor at all."

"So, Victor Boyd threatened you?" Miguel confirmed in a soft voice. Gloria nodded; her gaze still fixed on her hands.

The confirmation gave Gloria a motive.

Rosa yelled in the soundproof room. "She was eleven!"

Detective Sanchez shifted in his chair. "I'm afraid I'll have to ask you to speak for the sake of the recording, Miss Forrester."

Appearing fragile and childlike, Gloria swallowed then said, "Yes."

Miguel made a show of referring to his notes. "Miss Forrester, I understand that you were involved in parts building and electrical wiring at an aircraft plant during the war. Is that correct?"

Gloria pulled back; her forehead creased. "No. I was too young to work anywhere. Where did you hear that?"

Rosa sucked in a breath, knowing exactly where Miguel had heard the misinformation. She, herself, had told him that all the girls but Pauline and Marjorie worked at the aircraft plant during their school days. He had obviously taken it to mean Gloria as well.

Miguel made a note and then moved on to a new line of questioning.

"Miss Forrester, why did you check out a textbook on the electrician trade from the library?"

"Those were for Clarence! He knew I was going to the library and asked me to check them out."

Rosa's mind calculated this new information rapidly. Clarence wasn't anywhere near being on the suspect list. As far as she knew, he hadn't been to the fair that night. However, it wasn't like Rosa would necessarily have seen him if he had been. The boardwalk had been extremely crowded.

"For the sake of the recording," Detective Sanchez said, "Please state your relationship to Clarence Forrester."

"Clarence is my brother, older by two years," Gloria said. She narrowed her gaze at Miguel. "How did you know?"

"I visited the library today, Miss Forrester," Miguel said, "And checked out a textbook on electricity with your name in it myself."

If Rosa hadn't been put off her game by Miguel's unexpected presence, she would've continued looking for incriminating textbooks.

"Did Clarence say why he wanted that particular book?" Miguel asked.

"They were for our groundsman, Bernardo Diaz. The breakers in the electrical panel of the pool house kept tripping."

Miguel lifted his chin. "Why not just hire an electrician?"

"Bernardo insisted that he knew how to do it. He likes to call himself a 'Jack of all trades'. I think he's afraid of losing his job to someone more educated, but Mom would never fire him. He, Bledsoe, and Señora Gomez are like family. Clarence thought Bernardo might appreciate learning from a college textbook."

"And do a decent job in return," Miguel said.

Gloria nodded. "Exactly."

"Miss Forrester, you told your cousin, Rosa Reed, that you were going to the Surfside Lobster Bar at approximately eight p.m. last night, is that correct?"

In little more than a whisper, Gloria said, "That's what I told Rosa, yes."

Detective Sanchez glanced at Miguel before scribbling notes on a pad of paper.

Miguel continued, "But you didn't go there."

"No."

"Where did you go?"

Gloria glanced up at the window as if she knew Rosa was standing behind it. She hesitated a long moment, then answered. "At the boardwalk, I danced with a man I met from my ballroom dancing class. And well, we've grown fond of each other, and he's charming. After dancing together, he asked me if I wanted to go for a drive in his new convertible. I couldn't resist." She looked down at her lap again.

"And you went with this man?" Miguel confirmed.

"Yes. Yes, I did go with him."

"And what was this gentleman's name?" Miguel asked.

Again, Gloria glanced at the window. When she looked back at Miguel, she asked, "Do I have to say?"

"It would help prove your innocence in this case if we could place you somewhere else, Miss Forrester, and if this gentleman would vouch for your presence in his car when the murder was committed, you'd be free of all allegations."

Swallowing with difficulty, Gloria took a sip of her water before asking, "And who would find out what I tell you?"

"This conversation will go in my report. Who are you concerned will learn about it?"

Gloria still did not look up. "My mother."

"If we could confirm your alibi for last night, there would be no reason for us to share it with your mother," Miguel said.

Gloria finally raised her head. "His name is Alfred. Alfred Yang. I've only known him for a few weeks, but he's brilliant, and . . ."

Ah, now Rosa understood. Gloria liked a foreign man, and by the sound of his last name, he was Chinese, something Rosa knew keenly that Aunt Louisa wouldn't be able to tolerate. She and Miguel had once suffered because of her aunt's prejudices. How ironic that Miguel was the one questioning Gloria right now.

"I could never tell my mother," Gloria continued. "She would forbid it—more than that, she wouldn't look at me the same way again." She appealed to Miguel with earnestness. "This was the first time we've chanced meeting up anywhere together."

As if she suddenly remembered who was sitting next to her, Gloria gaped at Mr. Nabor with a new look of horror. "You can't tell her, can you?"

Mr. Nabor grunted. "Rest assured, Miss Forrester, you and I have lawyer-client privilege. I'm forbidden by law from mentioning anything said in this interview."

"Even though my mom is paying you?"

"Even so."

"To confirm for the record," Miguel said, "you were with this Mr. Alfred Yang the entire time you were apart from your cousin Rosa Reed? Would he attest to this?"

Gloria's head snapped toward Miguel. "You're not going to bring him in, are you?"

"I don't know if that will be necessary," Miguel said in an encouraging tone, but we will need to track down Mr. Yang at some point to corroborate your story. Can you tell us how we can get ahold of him?"

"Please, don't call his home. We're trying to keep this away from our families. At least for now." Gloria stared hard at Miguel. "Please?"

Miguel let out a short breath. "When is your next dance class, Miss Forrester?"

19

"I can't tell you how glad I am that is over," Gloria said, flopping back into the passenger seat of the Bel Air.

My sentiments exactly, Rosa thought as she turned on the ignition.

"Miguel let me watch from the other side of the glass. I hope you don't mind."

"I figured, and I'm glad. It might not have looked like it, but I imagined you behind the mirror, and I felt less alone." Gloria shook her shoulders and blew out a loud breath. "I feel surprisingly light, getting all of that out in the open."

"I'm sorry you were afraid to tell me about what Victor did to you." Rosa glanced away from the road just long enough so Gloria could see her sincerity. "It was so easy to be angry during the war. He directed his anger at everyone around him. It was like he was spraying them with a hose. I'm so sorry to hear you were caught in it."

"I wasn't alone. I haven't heard everyone's stories about Victor, but I'll bet there are more like mine."

Rosa turned the corner that led to the Forrester mansion. "Can you think of anyone who might be angry enough with Victor Boyd to go through with murder?"

Gloria shook her head, but then she stopped mid-shake. She turned to Rosa. "Wait. Do you remember when Marjorie first pointed out Victor at the fair?"

"Sure." Rosa nodded.

"And do you remember when Nancy Kline leaned over to whisper something to me?"

Rosa wasn't sure if she remembered that, but they'd just been reacquainted, and Rosa's thoughts were torn between their damaged friendship and Miguel's dynamic performance with his band. "I'm not sure. What did she whisper to you?"

"She said if she got the chance, she'd push Victor onto his roller coaster track. She said that would be exactly what he deserved, right there in the middle of the fair where everyone could see it." Gloria shook her head. "She was joking, though. She has an alibi, right?"

Rosa focused on the dimly lit road before her and let her thoughts go back to the night at the fair. Nancy had worn a baby-blue dress with a thick crinoline slip and danced with Eddie. Later, she sat with Pauline on the Ferris wheel.

"Does Nancy understand much about electricity or engineering?" Rosa asked. "Has Marjorie mentioned anything?" While Nancy had worked at the aircraft plant, Rosa didn't recall her being proficient. Besides, this was *Nancy*. Rosa just couldn't believe her old friend was capable of murder.

"Marjorie only talks about clothes and men," Gloria said with a scoff. "But Eddie's an electrician."

Rosa read little into that. A lot of men were electricians by trade, and probably many had been at the fair that night.

"So, tell me about this Alfred?" Rosa said it with a raised eyebrow so her cousin would know this was girl chat, not investigative work, and that Rosa wasn't judging. One day, she would tell Gloria about her long-ago romance with someone who most definitely wasn't approved by Aunt Louisa.

Gloria shrugged shyly, but once she opened her mouth, it seemed she was back to her old bubbly self. "I only met him a few weeks ago, so it's new, and it hasn't gone beyond a couple of conversations between dance routines. At class, I told him I was going to the Santa Bonita pier on Thursday night with my cousin, and did he want to meet me there. I wasn't sure what I was thinking." She rubbed her temples, and Rosa glimpsed the toll the evening had had on her cousin. "Then we happened to see each other at the bandstand, and somehow, the timing worked out perfectly with everyone else dancing so that I didn't have to say anything."

"And when he asked you to go for a drive, it just seemed easier not to mention it?" Rosa guessed. "That makes sense."

"Does it?" Gloria eyed Rosa, still looking for assurance.

Rosa reached over and took her hand. "Perfect sense."

WHEN ROSA and Gloria stepped out of the Bel Air, Aunt Louisa, Clarence, and Grandma Sally were out on the front stoop.

"What on earth was that all about?" Aunt Louisa braced her hands on her hips. "We've been worried sick!"

"It was nothing, Mom." Gloria stepped past Aunt Louisa and into the mansion. "A simple misunderstanding."

Aunt Louisa was incredulous. "A simple misunderstanding? Is that what you're calling it? You! Picked up by the police! Can you imagine the talk that will fly around town?" Aunt Louisa glowered at Rosa as if Gloria getting questioned by the police was her fault.

"They set her free, Mom," Clarence said with a tone of conciliation. "That means they didn't have anything to hold her."

Aunt Louisa shot daggers at her son. "Of course they didn't have anything!"

Gloria didn't stick around to engage in a second interrogation. Instead, she hurried up the stairs and left Rosa to face her aunt, Grandma Sally, and a defensive brother, alone.

"It really was a misunderstanding," Rosa said. "The police were simply doing their job."

"The mayor will hear about this!" Aunt Louisa spun on a heel of her leather pumps and click-clacked down the tile floors of the hallway.

"Louisa's experiencing enough fury for us all," Grandma Sally stated.

Despite her aunt's brash behavior toward him, Clarence came to his mother's defense. "She's just trying to protect the family name."

"Life is too short for long grievances." Grandma Sally smiled sardonically. "And I'm too old to be staying up this late. I bid you two young people goodnight."

Rosa eyed Clarence, who stood casually with his fists in his trouser pockets.

"What?" he said at last. "You're looking at me like I've got my hand in the cookie jar."

Rosa hated to admit to the thought that had crossed her mind. Had Clarence really wanted those library books for Bernardo's sake alone? Or did he have reason to brush up on his knowledge on how electrical circuits worked?

"Did you know Victor Boyd bullied Gloria when she was a child?"

Clarence stiffened. "What are you saying?"

"Gloria revealed to the police and to me, that Victor Boyd bullied her and stole a gold necklace. Were you aware of this?"

Clarence's lips tightened as red flared across his cheeks. He presented his fists and smacked one into the other. "I wasn't, but if I'd known, I'd have given him a knuckle sandwich. Done the dude in myself."

"Clarence!" Rosa admonished. "You really shouldn't say that. Not in the middle of a murder investigation."

Clarence looked decently chastised. "I didn't mean to rattle your cage, Rosa. I honestly didn't even know the guy." He wrinkled his nose. "You won't mention it to your cop friend, will ya?"

20

With a mother who owned a highbrow fashion shop, Rosa most often wore dresses. But there was the odd day when she'd wake up in the morning with a sixth sense in wardrobe decisions. Today was one such day. She dressed in a chartreuse pair of capri pants with a floral-patterned, collared blouse. She used a wide yellow headband to push her chestnut hair back and off her face.

As soon as she was dressed, Rosa phoned Miguel at the station. Unhappily, she felt it her duty to relay the threat Nancy Kline had uttered to Gloria about Victor Boyd. As Rosa had hoped, Miguel invited her to join him on his visit to the Klines.

With the windows down, and the radio on—she sang along with Patti Page's "How Much Is That Doggie In the Window?" giving Diego a quick apologetic look—

the drive through town was pleasant. Landmarks that had once felt like home, were welcoming again, like the bakery, the town hall, the brick fire hall, and the school, which now had a new extension. New buildings and businesses like Ralph's grocery and the Tastee Freeze ice cream parlor were feeling familiar as well.

Pushing her cat-eye sunglasses up along the bridge of her nose, Rosa cast a glance at Diego, who was partially inside the satchel sitting on the passenger seat of the Bel Air.

"Miguel didn't specifically ask for you to come," Rosa said. "However, if you behave and stay in the satchel, he might not notice."

Diego meowed and pushed his little paws against the edge of the satchel, and with his back legs worked himself out of the bag.

"Diego! What did I just say about behaving?"

Perhaps Diego had an issue with the song about the dog, as he jumped onto the dash, then reached down with one paw, patting at the radio dial.

"Get down!" Rosa said. "I'll turn it off."

Rosa switched the knob and the car grew quiet. "Are you happy now?"

Diego stretched out on the dash, sunning his furry stomach. Rosa laughed. "Oh, Diego, you have me in stitches."

When she pulled into the parking lot of the police station, Rosa reached for Diego and placed him back into the satchel. "It's time to be serious. Now remember, be cool."

Inside the station, Rosa told the policeman at the desk that Detective Belmonte was expecting her. He left, and soon afterward returned with Miguel on his heels.

Miguel took one look at her wriggling satchel—silly Diego just refused to cooperate—and frowned.

"After the emotional upheaval on display at the mansion last night, I didn't dare leave him behind," Rosa explained. "Aunt Louisa's on a rampage, and I fear for Diego's life, should he happen to cross her."

It was an overstatement but had the desired effect of gaining Miguel's sympathy. "I regret having to put you and your family through that."

"All in a day's work."

Miguel drove the unmarked police cruiser to a middle-class neighborhood on the other side of town and parked in front of a split-level house.

"This is where they live?" Rosa asked. She'd only ever been to Nancy's family home, which was far smaller and had housed a large family.

Miguel pushed the "three on the tree" gearshift into first and applied the park brake. "This is the address Sanchez dug up."

Rosa eased out of the vehicle, strapped her satchel over a shoulder, and felt Diego squirm inside. "Did you warn them we were coming?" she asked as they walked along the sidewalk and up the short driveway.

"No. In light of what your cousin Gloria told you last night, I thought a surprise visit might work in our favor."

Miguel knocked at the front door twice, and Rosa's stomach churned as they waited. Perhaps coming with Miguel was a mistake. Nancy would forever connect Rosa to what was sure to be an uncomfortable interview. Had Rosa had any hopes of mending fences, she was about to crush that possibility.

"Are you all right?" Miguel said.

"I don't know if you remember, but Nancy was my best friend when I last lived here."

Recollection dawned on Miguel, but before he could comment, the door opened, and Nancy stood before them, a look of curiosity on her face.

"Rosa?"

Miguel answered. "We're sorry to interrupt you. Is your husband home?"

"He's in the backyard with the kids." Nancy narrowed her gaze. "What's this about?"

"Just a few questions about the night of Mr. Boyd's death," Miguel replied. "We're speaking with all the witnesses."

"We're hardly witnesses. We didn't see a thing."

"You might've seen something without realizing it," Rosa added. "Something that will help us. Detective Belmonte only needs a few moments."

Evoking the authority of Miguel's position did the trick, and Nancy waved to the sidewalk that wrapped around the house. "Follow that path to the gate and let yourselves in. We're in the middle of a game of croquet."

Croquet? Rosa wondered. Croquet was a popular sport in England, and the thought of the game gave Rosa a small pang for home. She had no idea that Americans played it as well.

Rosa followed Miguel to a path along the side of the house, and sure enough, on the sprawling back lawn were several croquet hoops arranged in a course. Eddie Kline stood with three young boys who were staggered in height. Each held a mallet.

Miguel and Rosa stepped through the waist-high gate in time to see Nancy conferring with her husband. Eddie cast them a look of distrust. He then announced to his sons, "Fifteen-minute break, boys. Go get yourselves some lemonade in the kitchen."

"I'm Detective Belmonte with the Santa Bonita Police Department," Miguel started, "and I believe you know Miss Reed. She's an officer with the London Metropolitan Police and is acting with our local department as a special consultant."

Eddie shot Rosa a look and lifted his chin. "Hey, Rosa."

"Hi, Eddie," Rosa said. She'd seen Eddie at the fair, but they hadn't had a chance to speak, not that they'd ever truly been friends.

Arms folded over her chest, Nancy's impatience stormed across her face. Rosa imagined that her former friend was holding back on tapping her foot. "You wanted to ask us about the night Victor died?"

"To confirm," Miguel said, "you were both at the boardwalk when Victor Boyd died, correct?"

"Yes. An unfortunate accident," Nancy muttered.

Nancy wouldn't consider the loss of Victor Boyd unfortunate, Rosa thought.

"Actually," Miguel said, "we've escalated the cause of death to murder." He let that sink in.

Nancy and Eddie shared worried looks.

"If you wouldn't mind," Miguel continued, his gaze on Eddie, "I'd like to ask you a few questions in private, Mr. Kline."

Rosa turned to Nancy. "Perhaps we could have a cup of tea."

Nancy laughed without mirth. "Only if you want it cold. This isn't England."

Rosa didn't blame Nancy for being brash and defensive and took the snub in her stride.

Inside, the boys were engaged in a raucous game of cowboys and scrambled about the house making shooting noises. "*Bang, bang!*"

Nancy yelled with little effect. "No running in the house." Then to Rosa. "We can close the door to the kitchen and get a little peace there."

Compared to the kitchen at the Forrester mansion, Nancy's kitchen would be considered cozy with its green walls and white cabinetry. But small. Then again, any room of most homes when compared to the mansion would be small.

Rosa took a seat

Nancy pulled down on the handle of a single-door, new-model Frigidaire to reveal the contents inside. She removed a pitcher that clamored for space beside a half dozen glass bottles of milk, then kicked the door closed with her foot.

Nancy spoke as she poured two glasses of lemonade. "You can't be having much of a vacation with all the gumshoeing you've been doing since you got back."

Rosa accepted her glass and took a grateful sip. "Once a copper always a copper."

Nancy grinned. "Copper, huh? That's swell."

Rosa was grateful for the smile.

At that moment, Diego's cute little fuzzy face poked out of the satchel.

"Is your cat thirsty?"

"If you don't mind a dish of water for him, that would be dandy."

"Water? Phooey!" Nancy plucked a bottle of milk from the refrigerator and poured a little into a small bowl. As she set it on the floor beside Rosa's feet, Rosa removed Diego from her bag and placed him on the floor. He eagerly lapped up the milk.

"Thanks," Rosa said.

"I like cats, but Eddie's allergic, so we can't have one."

"Is it all right that Diego's here?"

"Oh, a few sneezes won't kill him." Nancy put the milk away then took one of the speckled vinyl chairs at the Formica-topped table. "So, Officer Reed. Fire away,"

"It's just a matter of form," Rosa said lightly. "You know, crossing all the t's and dotting all the i's"

A crash from the other room caught Nancy's attention. "Fine, but let's hurry it up before my boys tear the house apart."

"They're handsome," Rosa said. "You must be proud."

Nancy relaxed. "They're a handful, but I love them. Can't imagine life without them now. Sorry I didn't introduce you to them properly."

"Another time," Rosa said, then gently asked, "Did you say that if you got the chance, you would push Victor onto his roller coaster track?"

Nancy's face went pale. She shook her head. "I didn't mean it. Did Gloria tell you that? It's not what I meant!"

"What did you mean?"

"Oh, I don't know. It was just talk. I wouldn't *kill* anyone. Rosa, you know me."

Rosa patted Nancy's hand. "I know."

"Besides, I was with Marjorie and Pauline on another ride when it happened."

"Eddie's an electrician now?" Rosa said.

Nancy answered tentatively. "Yes . . . I know Victor died from an electrical mishap, but Eddie wasn't even in the park at that time. He had an early shift the next day, and had to come home to relieve my mother, who was babysitting. I told you that in the park."

Rosa nodded, remembering. "Like I said, we needed to speak with you and Eddie as a matter of form."

Nancy rubbed a finger through the wet ring of condensation on the table left behind by her glass. "I can vouch for Marjorie, so you don't have to bother her. But I can't say what Pauline was doing. Although, she's got a lot of technical engineering knowledge, so you might want to talk to her."

"Oh?"

"You remember," Nancy stared at Rosa with meaning. "Pauline Van Peridon of the practically famous Santa Bonita Van Peridons? Robert Van Peridon, Pauline's father, was the founder of the Aeronautical Research Center," Nancy explained, "which put Santa Bonita on the map—what with its technological developments in radar."

Now that Nancy mentioned it, Rosa recalled that Mr. Van Peridon had died at the end of the war in a traffic accident.

"Did you know that Marjorie is interested in Henry Van Peridon?"

Nancy's brow collapsed. "What makes you say that?"

"I saw them together a couple of times. The way they look at each other—"

"Ah, that's a bunch of hooey. If Marjorie was romantically interested in someone, she would've told me. She always tells me about her crushes." Nancy's lips tugged upward. "Even when I don't want to hear about them. Besides, I think the older brother, Thomas, would be more her style."

"Oh?"

"Henry's a little on the small side. Marjorie's tall and she goes for the stronger type.

The way Nancy was so certain made Rosa question Marjorie's motives. Despite her mild denials, Marjorie had definitely shown interest in Henry Van Peridon, or at least pretended to, so why was she keeping it a secret from her sister? Did she really like Henry and didn't want to deal with Nancy's surprise? Or was she using Henry to gain information about how to rig the electrical panel at the fair?

"Pauline has been working at the center ever since," Nancy continued, "and understands electrical wiring and technology better than any person I know, man or woman."

The memories came flooding back—Victor Boyd pushing Pauline out the school doors during a school blackout. Victor Boyd spouting off that the real heroes put themselves on the front lines. Those that hid at home, he'd said, 'playing with switches and wires', deserved to be marched in front of a firing line.

At the time, Rosa had felt bad for Victor—he had been kind to her and had lost his dad. But now, she knew he hadn't lost his dad in the war. His dad had been in prison while Pauline Van Peridon's father was making headlines with his work helping the war effort. It was clear why Victor had picked on Pauline so extensively, and so cruelly, that to this day, she could barely bring herself to speak.

Pauline Van Peridon had motive. She had means. She had opportunity.

21

After a stop at the police station, and a phone call later, Rosa learned from Miguel that the Aeronautical Research Center was a family affair with Pauline working as manager of Testing and Research and her two brothers, Thomas and Henry, heading engineering.

The research center rested in the hills at the north end of Santa Bonita. Rosa, with Diego squirming in the satchel beside her, sat in the back seat of the cruiser, Miguel sat in the passenger seat, and Detective Sanchez drove the vehicle along the winding incline. If a person didn't already know the research center was there, it was entirely possible to be ignorant of its existence.

"The center was started by Robert Van Peridon," Miguel said, casting a glance over his shoulder at Rosa. "Unfortunately, he was killed in a hit and run during a freak storm. The rain washed away any evidence of the vehicle responsible, and the perpetrator was never apprehended. Since the war was nearly over, the press spun the story as a last-ditch effort by the enemy to take out some of America's most essential advancement forerunners."

"How awful," Rosa said. "The Van Peridon children are orphans."

Detective Sanchez, with a dry cigarette hanging from the corner of his mouth, grunted. "They inherited their old man's company and his money."

"Are you suggesting one of them ran their own father down?" Rosa asked.

"The driver was never caught, so who's to say?"

They reached an imposing security gate with a warning sign written in both English and Spanish meant to frighten off trespassers. A guard emerged from a hut to greet them. Detective Sanchez and Miguel flashed their badges.

"We'd like to have a few words with a Miss Pauline Van Peridon," Miguel announced.

The guard didn't say a word, only nodded and returned to the security hut. Through the window, Rosa could see the man pick up the receiver of a telephone and dial. Several drawn-out moments later, he emerged to say, "I'm afraid Miss Van Peridon isn't available today."

"Not available, or not here?" Miguel asked. "This is

official police business, and I must insist that she presents herself if she is on the premises."

The guard glanced to his upper right, a possible sign that he was about to lie. Reading facial expressions and body language was a skill Rosa had learned from her mother. The guard glanced back at Miguel and said, "She's not here today."

Miguel nodded. "And do you know where we can find her?"

The guard shook his head.

Rosa muttered from the backseat, "Whoever's in charge."

"We'd like to go in and have a chat with whoever is in charge on the premises today," Miguel said as he flashed his badge again.

The guard made another call, and moments later announced, "Mr. Tom Van Peridon will meet you there." He rolled the gate open and directed them down the rest of the driveway to the parking lot.

Rosa adjusted the bobby pin that held her bangs out of her eyes and peered at the man who stood waiting for them. She knew what Henry looked like, and this man wasn't him. She surmised that it must be the eldest brother, Thomas Van Peridon. Like Nancy had claimed, this brother was taller and built like a soldier. He wore a blue shirt and yellow tie, gray slacks, and a straw fedora.

The building behind Tom Van Peridon looked more like the spaceships Rosa had seen in comic books when she was young than any building she'd been to in real life. The roof was sleek, slanted metal and angled low to the ground on all sides. Rosa suspected much of the center operated underground, hidden away.

"Why don't you two see what you can get out of Mr. Van Peridon," Rosa said. "Perhaps you can convince him to take you inside. Insist on meeting Henry Van Peridon. Tell them I'm an arrest—you were just on your way back to the station with me. Insinuate that I'm cuffed and harmless. Leave me in the car."

Without looking back, Miguel said, "What are you thinking?"

"It'll give me a chance to look around. And if I'm caught, I'll just play the weak female card and say I'm lost. Maybe I can find Pauline."

Miguel worked his lips. "I don't know."

"Could be dangerous," Detective Sanchez added as he parked and killed the engine. Tom Van Peridon would be able to see into the car, but not well.

"I'm only looking for Pauline," Rosa said. "I think I can handle her." She was about to remind the men that she, too, had police training and could take care of herself, but then Miguel opened the glove compartment, pulled out a pair of metal handcuffs, and slid them over the back of his seat.

"Be careful, Rosa," he said. "I mean it."

Then, without another word, Miguel and Sanchez got out of the car and approached Pauline's brother.

Rosa debated what to do next. She glanced at the handcuffs. Where was the key?

Miguel had forgotten to give her the key. She decided to lock up her left arm and gently placed the other side over her right wrist without clicking it into place.

And just in time!

The second her hands were back on her lap, she looked up to see a fourth man—slight in build with dark hair greased straight back—at the passenger window, looking in.

Henry Van Peridon.

Rosa didn't think Henry would recognize her. She'd only ever seen him from a distance, but as a precaution, she kept her gaze averted and her head turned. He seemed more concerned with the handcuffs on her wrists, and moments later, slapped the roof before walking away.

Joining his brother, Henry and Thomas conferred with Miguel and Detective Sanchez for several minutes, far enough from the police vehicle that Rosa couldn't hear what they were saying. Miguel regularly motioned toward the building, and the two men responded with shaking heads. It wasn't difficult to understand the nature of the conversation. Soon Miguel motioned in the other direction where Rosa now saw a path that likely led to the back of the building. A flat metal blade angling through some trees was just visible from her point of view and looked like it could be a part of an airplane.

The moment the men rounded the corner of the building, Rosa grabbed the car door handle, carefully opened the door, and then closed it behind her. She stared back at Diego through the window, his little face with his big golden eyes staring up with a look of betrayal.

"Sorry, Diego. I've got to go alone this time. I'll be back as soon as I can."

Keeping low to the ground, Rosa crept away from the police car toward the building. The overhang of the low-slanted roof shadowed the front entrance. Not until she neared the glass doors did she see a bored-looking security guard wearing brown pants and a tan shirt stretched over a round belly.

She pressed against the building then snuck in the opposite direction from where the men had gone. Several metal, windowless doors lined the side of the building, but they were all locked, and for all Rosa knew, they could have been guarded on the other side. Reaching the backside of the building, she came to a cliff front. Rosa now understood why they had built the research center here. Only three sides could be breached.

Directly above her, where the building protruded out over the cliff, was a large balcony. It had wall-to-wall windows and a glass door out onto it. Rosa was glad she'd chosen to wear capri pants rather than a dress, as some climbing would be required. She scanned the rock face under the balcony for the best place to find hold, slipped out of her sandals, and heaved herself onto a wooden crossbar. Like her mother, Rosa was stronger than she looked. As she hoisted herself up and found her footing, she thought back to the times while on duty that she'd climbed fire escapes or alley fences to catch a running suspect. The same adrenaline ran through her veins now.

It wasn't a tall building, and she only had to make less than fifteen feet. Hand over hand, and ignoring the weight of the handcuff hanging from her left arm, she climbed the braces of the overhang one by one. When she reached the railing, she carefully maneuvered over it and found herself on solid footing.

The sunshine beat down on the window and made it difficult to see through. For a split second, Rosa thought she was looking into a mirror rather than through a plate of glass. Reflected was a slender woman with brown hair, but this one wasn't wearing capri pants. This one wore a blue dress.

"Pauline!" Rosa yelled through the glass. "I just want to ask—" But she stopped because Pauline had already spun and raced out a door behind her.

22

The balcony door was open with only a screen door blocking Rosa's way. With more strength than was necessary, Rosa whipped it open and stepped inside.

The family office? Three large mahogany desks were covered with everything from paperwork to wires and knobs and steel plates. Rosa approached the first one and noted a framed black-and-white photograph of a man dressed in a suit with baggy pants and a double-breasted jacket, and a fedora hat styled from the war years. An inscription plate attached to the frame read, Robert Van Peridon, 1901-1945. He stood proudly by an old wartime airplane.

An item sitting close to the photo stopped Rosa in her tracks. A cylindrical piece of red rubber, with a jagged open slice down one side, sat on the ledge beside the photo as though it were a trophy. A shiver went down Rosa's spine.

The lever for the roller coaster's brake.

Rosa raced to the office door and opened it a sliver to peek at what was on the other side. A grouping of glass-paneled rooms as far as the eye could see. Workers in lab coats filled the spaces, and there were walls upon walls of buttons and interconnected wires and flashing lights. A female figure gestured madly at a security guard.

Rosa hesitated. If she scaled back down the balcony trestles, she would never catch Pauline, but if she went the faster way, down the stairs and out the front door, the security guard was sure to stop her.

Or try to.

Keeping her eyes peeled for anything that might assist her, Rosa raced from the office and down the hall toward the stairs. The researchers paid her no attention, which was helpful. As she passed the third glass-walled room, she saw *exactly* what she needed hanging from a hook by the door. *A spare lab coat*!

It was big on her, which would help conceal the handcuffs still dangling from her left wrist. Nobody seemed to notice her grab the smock or race for the stairs while slipping her arms inside.

She didn't look the part of a tidy researcher. Her hair had fallen slightly forward and her feet were bare, but she hoped that if she strode past the security guard with purpose, as though she knew exactly where she was going and what she was doing, he would pay her little attention.

As she reached the main floor, Rosa took in a breath and confidently strode for the front door, but as she passed the guard, he called to her.

"Hey!"

Rosa sprinted away, and as she hoped, the rotund guard didn't have the endurance to keep up with her. Dodging tables and startling scientists, she pushed through the glass door of the exit and into the bright sun.

Cupping her eyes against the glare, she searched the parking lot for movement.

If Pauline got away from the research center, who knew how long she could hide from them? By the looks of this research center, she probably had enough money to stay hidden for the rest of her life if she wanted—she was smart enough to do it too.

Movement along the side of the building caught Rosa's attention. A silver Buick, as unmemorable as Pauline's fashion sense, backed quickly out of a parking space. Rosa, hearing the loud puffing of the security guard behind her, broke into a run. As her bare feet hit pebbles sticking out of the asphalt, Rosa winced but didn't stop until she was right in front of Pauline's car. She slapped her hands on the hood of the vehicle, the handcuffs making a loud *clank*.

Pauline shouted out of the open window. "Get out of the way, Rosa! Please!"

The security guard had stopped several paces back, winded and bent over, his thick arms bracing his knees.

Rosa stared hard at Pauline through the windshield and showed every ounce of her determination. There were only two choices here for Pauline: Run over Rosa, or give herself up.

"Please, Rosa! You don't understand. He killed our dad!"

Rosa relaxed her hold on the hood of the car. "Who killed your dad?"

"Victor. Victor Boyd." Pauline, the quiet one, had found her voice now. "When I saw him at the boardwalk, I only meant to tell him off for how he'd treated me in school." She sobbed into the sleeve of her blouse. "He laughed in my face then told me that he was the one who'd run my dad down."

"Don't tell them anything else, Paulie!" Tom Van Peridon's voice reached them from behind.

Rosa turned to see his long, skinny legs move with surprising speed toward them.

"They don't have anything," he said, "Just keep your mouth shut."

Miguel and Detective Sanchez raced out of the building with Henry Van Peridon on their heels. Grabbing Tom by the arm, Miguel pulled him back so he couldn't go near his sister.

Pauline sniffed. "I thought maybe Victor was lying, just trying to upset me because he was upset, but . . ."

Slowly, Rosa made her way to the driver's door, reached over Pauline, and turned off the car's ignition.

"And you couldn't let it go?" Rosa pushed gently.

Pauline shook her head and spoke to the steering wheel. "Victor Boyd, more than anybody in this world, deserved payback. But, Rosa, I didn't kill him. He was alive and carrying that stupid pole when I left him."

Rosa had a gut feeling Pauline was telling the truth. But if she hadn't killed him . . .

Pauline was a testing and research manager and wouldn't know how to rig the panel for the roller coaster, at least not within the limited amount of time she would have had.

But her brothers were electrical engineers. Either of them would know how.

The question now was, who was Pauline trying to protect?

"Pauline," Rosa said gently, "If you're innocent, why did you run from me?"

Pauline's tear-filled eyes glanced at her brother Henry. When Rosa followed her gaze, Miguel and Detective Sanchez did the same.

Unlike his brother, Henry buckled under pressure. He darted into the surrounding forest, his actions all but confirming his guilt.

Miguel took off after him. "Henry Van Peridon, stop!"

Rosa stared at Detective Sanchez, who made a show of holding Tom Van Peridon, and not easily.

Pauline wasn't a real danger, and Miguel was about to disappear into the forest without backup. Rosa hurried after him.

Her pulse raced, not only because of the adrenaline rush that came from the chase but because Miguel could be in danger. For all they knew, Henry Van Peridon could have set booby-traps around the research center.

Rosa didn't spend a lot of time barefoot, and despite the urgency of the situation, the pain that shot up her legs from pokey twigs and sharp pebbles slowed her down.

"Miguel!"

It was too quiet. Rosa fought against the pain in her feet and kept running. "Miguel!"

Please, Lord, let him be all right.

She pushed through the scraggly desert brush, wincing at the scratches inflicted on her forearms. "Miguel?"

She broke into a clearing and stopped short. Straddling Henry Van Peridon, who was lying facedown on the dirt, was Miguel, holding his captive's arms tight behind his back.

Rosa took a moment to catch her breath. The thought of something happening to Miguel, of *losing* him, was an incredible ache, and she soaked in the feeling of immense relief she felt at seeing he was alive and well.

Oblivious to the gamut of emotion Rosa was

wrestling still, Miguel nodded to the handcuff weighing painfully from her wrist. "You done with those?"

"I need a key."

"Ah, right." Miguel put pressure on Mr. Van Peridon's back with one hand. With the other, he retrieved the handcuff key from his pocket and handed it to Rosa.

Rosa freed herself then watched as Miguel snapped them on Mr. Van Peridon's wrists.

"Nice work, Detective Belmonte," Rosa said, unable to keep from grinning.

Miguel's copper-brown eyes focused on hers, and adorable dimples formed.

Rosa held in a sigh. The man still made her quiver.

"Same to you, WPC Reed."

23

Riding her Schwinn bicycle down the wide street leading to the Kline residence, Rosa slowed to a stop in front of their house.

She hadn't called ahead. What if Nancy was busy? Or worse, what if she never wanted to see Rosa again?

One of the curtain panels in the living room moved, and Rosa saw Nancy's perplexed expression as she stared out. Soon afterward, the front door opened.

"Are you spying on me?"

"No. Why would I do that?"

"Oh, I dunno. Some cop thing, maybe."

"I'm off duty," Rosa said with a smile. She wasn't actually on the force there, so she was as much of a civilian as Nancy was.

"Well, come in, why doncha? You're making me nervous."

Nancy stood on her front steps and watched Rosa park her bike in the driveway.

"Don't tell me you brought that cat again?"

Rosa was just about to lift the satchel holding Diego out of the basket. "Oh, I forgot about Eddie's allergies. Should I come back later?"

Nancy flicked a palm dismissively. "Nah. He's at work. Bring the critter inside. But I must warn you; the boys are home."

Evidence of that statement was clear. Forts made from sheets filled the living room with the boys crawling rambunctiously between them. One of the sheets covered a lamp, and Nancy got there just in time to save the ornamental piece before it crashed to the floor. "That's enough! Outside with you! It's a nice day. You should be outside."

"Aw, Mom!"

Nancy pointed to the back door. "Go. I have company."

Chugging like a train out of coal, the three boys slumped out of the room with droopy shoulders.

Nancy wiped her brow. "It's the summer holidays. I, for one, can't wait for school to start again."

"I should've rung first."

"Rang what?'

"I mean, I should've called first."

"Oh well, you're here now." Nancy placed a hand on the hip over her full skirt. "Why?"

Rosa blinked at her bluntness. "I've come to apologize."

Nancy hummed. "That calls for a drink, I suppose. There's iced tea in the fridge."

Rosa followed Nancy to the kitchen, and just like the last time, Nancy provided a little bowl of milk for Diego. Rosa somehow missed Nancy's sleight of hand as she poured the iced tea, because her first sip was a shock.

Nancy chuckled. "I spiked it a little. The boys know not to touch Mommy's tea."

Knowing what she was in for now, Rosa took another sip. "Thank you."

Nancy simply nodded and waited for Rosa to do what she'd come for.

"I'm sorry I stopped writing to you, Nancy."

Nancy's shoulders slumped, and her hand went to the lace collar at her neck. "You were my best pen pal. I thought we'd be writing to each other forever."

"Me too, but . . ."

"What happened?" Nancy took a sip of her drink

"It's going to sound selfish and stupid."

Nancy smirked. "Hey, I'm married to Eddie Kline!"

"Point taken. The last letter I wrote to Miguel came back return to sender." She glanced up at Nancy and held her gaze. "You know how much I loved him, and my heart was broken so terribly when I thought he'd given up. Like I said, I was young and stupid and assumed the worst. The army probably had relocated him, and my mail didn't get properly redirected." Rosa paused and took another fortifying sip of tea.

"Did you ask him about it?" Nancy asked.

Rosa nearly choked on her tea. "No way. Water under the bridge, as they say. He's got a new love."

"Why should that stop you?"

"Nancy!"

"I'm just saying. If this were an episode of *As the World Turns*, you'd be marching up to his door and confessing your unfailing love."

Rosa wasn't the sort who'd knowingly break up the relationship of another couple, and this was her *real* life, not scripted entertainment!

"If I marched up to his door to do anything, it would be to apologize, just like I'm trying to do now with you."

"Oh, right. Get on with it, then."

Outside, Rosa could hear one of the boys shouting, "Bang, bang, you're dead!"

Nancy rose and closed the window.

"What I'm trying to say," Rosa started, "was that when I stopped writing to Miguel, I found it hard to pen a normal letter to you. I had a wastebasket full of my attempts, believe me, but everything I wrote . . . well, the truth was so maudlin, and truthfully, my life was a bore. You were writing about your wedding and your new baby, and I was just pathetic."

"Oh, Rosa," Nancy said. Her blue eyes flashed

with sympathy. "Men—you can't live with them, and you can't live without them."

Rosa inhaled deeply and forced a smile. "Anyway, I'm here now and ready to move forward."

"Are you going to tell me about *Lord* Winston Eveleigh?"

The way she emphasized the word "Lord" made Rosa laugh. "Let's save that for another day."

Nancy raised her glass.

"And another glass of Mommy's tea."

They tapped their glasses together in a small toast.

Rosa broached the next item on her list. "How is Marjorie?"

Tom and Pauline Van Peridon had been released on bail for charges of obstruction of justice and would likely pay a fine or serve a few days of community service.

Henry Van Peridon, on the other hand, remained locked up in the local jail awaiting trial. The rubber sheath Rosa had discovered was covered with Victor's prints, which confirmed it had come from the scene of the crime. The forensics team had found a partial print belonging to Henry on the control panel of the roller coaster as he'd done a poor job, with his limited time, of trying to rub them out. There were also prints on the rubber sheath, however, Henry hadn't guessed that would be found.

Shortly after Pauline's encounter with Victor, she'd told Henry what she'd learned. Waiting until Pauline went home, Henry obtained tools he had stored in his car, and after waiting for a moment of opportunity, sabotaged the roller coaster, ensuring Victor Boyd's electrocution and death.

"She's furious," Nancy replied. "At Henry for being a murderer and not being able to marry her and make her the wife of someone with money and esteem, and at herself for being gullible. I can't believe she didn't tell me what she was thinking."

"Better she learn the truth about him now," Rosa said.

"That's what I told her and it got me a pillow in the face."

GLORIA WAS WAITING for Rosa when she arrived at the Forrester mansion. "I forgot to give this to you this morning." She handed Rosa a single envelope. "I hope it's not important."

The envelope had a postage stamp with the image of the Queen on it. Rosa's heart jumped at the prospect of getting a letter from her parents, but when she saw the handwriting, her heart sank.

"What is it?" Gloria said. "You look pale."

"It's nothing," Rosa said, forcing cheer into her voice. She offered her satchel to her cousin. "Do you mind watching him for a little while?"

Gloria happily took Diego, and Rosa headed upstairs to her room. Thankful for the Long Island iced tea still in her veins, Rosa sat at her desk, took a deep breath, and ripped the envelope with a letter opener.

It was from Winston. Of course, he wouldn't bother to ring her. She sighed. He probably feared she wouldn't have accepted his call, and he was probably right.

My dearest Rosa,

I hope this letter finds you well. I'll keep it short and to the point.

I forgive you. Come home, and we'll forget about this childish nonsense. You are my betrothed. Since large ceremonies obviously frighten you, we'll keep it small. A little country church will suffice. I've found one in Charlton and have already confirmed a date next month with the vicar. No need to worry about the local gossips. The European Cup Final in Paris is all anyone can talk about now.

I've included your return ticket.

See you soon, darling,

Yours, Winston

A second look in the envelope did provide the ticket. How presumptuous! Rosa found a pad of paper in the desk along with a ballpoint pen. An idea had rattled in her head for a couple of days, but it wasn't until she'd received this letter that she knew what she wanted to do.

DEAR WINSTON,

Thank you for your letter, and I hope this one finds you well. Like you, I'll get straight to the point. I'm afraid I must decline. I've decided I'm going to stay in California for an indeterminate amount of time.

I can't marry you. My returning to London at this point would make life too difficult for both of us. We must, each of us, move on with our lives.

Please, once again, accept my sincerest apologies.

SINCERELY,

Rosa

AFTER DELIVERING her letter to Señora Gomez with instructions to add it to the outgoing mail, Rosa headed to Uncle Harold's old office to use the telephone.

Pleased to see that Aunt Louisa was absent, Rosa closed the door to ensure privacy. Checking her watch for the time, she saw that it was too late for her to ring London. She had something to tell her parents, but it would have to wait until the morning.

Besides, she had another call to make.

Feeling nervous, Rosa dialed the morgue before she lost her nerve.

"Hello, Larry," she said when Dr. Rayburn answered. "I hope you don't mind that I called you. Are you still interested in going on a date?"

The End

ROSA & MIGUEL'S WARTIME ROMANCE

PREQUEL - EXCERPT

If you enjoyed reading *Murder on the Boardwalk* please help others enjoy it too.

Recommend it: Help others find the book by recommending it to friends, readers' groups, discussion boards and by **suggesting it to your local library.**

Review it: Please tell other readers why you liked this book by reviewing it on Amazon or Goodreads.

Eager to read the next book in the Rosa Reed Mystery series?

Don't miss MURDER AT THE BOMB SHELTER.

Murder's a blast!

Rosa Reed's holiday with the Forester Family in Santa Bonita has turned into an extended stay, and Rosa decides to make use of her Metropolitan Police training and sets up a private investigative business ~ just like her mother! But she finds she's not the only one who keeps business in the family, and when one of the members of the prestigious Gainer family is found dead in his bomb shelter, Rosa is invited to take on the case ~ much to Detective Miguel Belmonte's chagrin. If Rosa doesn't find the killer soon, the summer of '56 just might be her last.

Buy on AMAZON or read for free with Kindle Unlimited!

Read on for a sneak peek.

Did you read the PREQUEL?

Rosa & Miguel's Wartime Romance is a BONUS short story exclusively for Lee's newsletter subscribers.

How it All Began. . .

Like many British children during World War Two, Rosa Reed's parents, Ginger and Basil Reed, made the heart-wrenching decision to send their child to a foreign land and out of harm's way. Fortunately, Ginger's half-sister Louisa and her family, now settled in the quaint coastal town of Santa Bonita, California, were pleased to take her in.

By the spring of 1945, Rosa Reed had almost made it through American High School unscathed, until the American army decided to station a base there. Until she met the handsome Private Miguel Belmonte and fell in love. . .

Visit leestraussbooks.com to claim your copy.

Rosa Reed first laid eyes on Miguel Belmonte on the fourteenth day of February in 1945. She was a senior attending a high school dance, and he a soldier who played in the band.

She'd been dancing with her date, Tom Hawkins, a short, stalky boy with pink skin and an outbreak of acne, but her gaze continued to latch onto the bronze-skinned singer, with dark crew-cut hair, looking very dapper in a black suit.

In a life-changing moment, their eyes locked. Despite the fact that she stared at the singer over the shoulder of her date, she couldn't help the bolt of electricity that shot through her, and when the singer smiled—and those dimples appeared—heavens, her knees almost gave out!

"Rosa?"

Tom's worried voice brought her back to reality. "Are you okay? You went a little limp there. Do you feel faint? It is mighty hot in here." Tom released Rosa's hand to tug at his tie. "Do you want to get some air?"

Rosa felt a surge of alarm. Invitations to step outside the gymnasium were often euphemisms to get fresh.

In desperation she searched for her best friend Nancy Davidson—her best *American* friend, that was. Vivien Eveleigh claimed the position of *best* friend back in London, and Rosa missed her. Nancy made for a sufficient substitute. A pretty girl with honey-blond hair, Nancy, fortunately, was no longer dancing, and was sitting alone.

"I think I'll visit the ladies, Tom, if you don't mind."

He looked momentarily put out, then shrugged. "Suit yourself." He joined a group of lads—boys—at the punch table, and joined in with their raucous laughter. Rosa didn't want to know what they were joking about, or at whose expense.

Nancy understood Rosa's plight as she wasn't entirely pleased with her fellow either. "If only you and I could dance with each other."

"One can't very well go to a dance without a date, though," Rosa said.

Nancy laughed. "*One* can't."

Rosa rolled her eyes. Even after four years of living in America, her Englishness still manifested when she was distracted.

And tonight's distraction was the attractive lead singer in the band, and shockingly, he seemed to have sought her face out too.

Nancy had seen the exchange and gave Rosa a firm nudge. "No way, José. I know he's cute, but he's from the wrong side of the tracks. Your aunt would have a conniption."

Nancy wasn't wrong about that. Aunt Louisa had very high standards, as one who was lady of Forrester mansion, might.

"I'm only looking!"

Nancy harrumphed. "As long as it stays that way."

Continue reading >>>

Rosa & Miguel's Wartime Romance is a BONUS short story exclusively for Lee's newsletter subscribers.

Visit **leestraussbooks.com** to claim your copy.

MURDER AT THE BOMB SHELTER SNEAK PEEK

CHAPTER ONE

Rosa Reed peddled her Schwinn *Deluxe Hollywood* bicycle down the boulevard on another sunny Santa Bonita, California day. As she breathed in the sweet scent of sage and saline, she briskly rode down the slight incline toward *Ron's New and Used Cars.* Over the last few weeks, she'd ridden by often, but today her heart fluttered with excitement as she approached the business establishment.

Yesterday, while heading home from a short shopping trip with her kitten Diego—who rode in the front basket with his fuzzy face into the wind—she spied a new arrival on the car lot. She simply *had* to stop for a look. That polo-white, two-door 1953 Chevrolet Corvette Roadster convertible with red leather interior had gripped her imagination, and at that moment, Rosa fell in love.

One of only three hundred made that year, the

automobile, with its serial number of #76, was already considered a collector's item. Rosa had slid into the red leather seat with Diego safely tucked into her satchel. When she'd revved the engine, the frame rumbled, and the powerful sound roared through the tailpipe, causing her to smile mischievously.

With the top down, she'd test-driven the vehicle, riding north onto the Pacific Coast Highway—a warm August breeze mussing her short brown hair. She'd allowed herself a moment of thrill when she pressed harder on the accelerator. *My mother would love this car*! The thought made her laugh out loud as she thundered past the city limits sign, swirls of dust whipping in her disappearing wake.

Upon returning to the lot, Rosa immediately phoned her Aunt Louisa, the matriarch of the Forrester mansion, to arrange for temporary financing until she could get the money wired from the London bank that held her trust fund.

"I'm part of the Forrester family," she'd told the dealer. "I'll be back tomorrow if you'd be kind enough to hold it for me."

By the look of respect at the mention of the Forrester family name—and perhaps a little fear, after all, Aunt Louisa's reputation in the town was formidable—the dealer promised to hold it.

Now, as Rosa signed the papers for ownership and registration, anticipation rushed through her. The days that lay ahead of her! Her recent decision to stay in

Santa Bonita and set up a private investigation office instead of returning to her job as a police officer in London was further cemented with the purchase of this car.

"You don't mind stowing my bicycle for a day or so . . ." Rosa said, her voice a lively lilt. ". . . until I can arrange for it to be picked up."

"Not at all, Miss Reed," the dealer said with a firm handshake and a grin as sparkling as Santa Bonita bay.

Minutes later, Diego safely ensconced in her large satchel, Rosa pointed the Corvette toward the business district. She'd remembered to bring a silk headscarf, the same pink color of her lipstick—her mother would approve—so her hair stayed neatly in place. A pair of gray-and-green Polaroid tortoise sunglasses sat on her nose, and she steered her new steed along the roadway with gloved hands.

She congratulated herself for staying in the right-hand lane. Rosa had learned to drive in America during the war years when she'd been shipped out of London to the safety her Aunt Louisa had offered. Shifting her inclination to drive on the left was like riding a bike. Having a steering wheel on the left-hand side, rather than the right, helped with reorientation.

Shortly afterward, Rosa parked her Corvette along the curb in front of an office. Now standing by the building's front door, she paused to admire her new car before stepping inside. Diego meowed softly from his spot inside a designer pink-and-yellow striped satchel that matched Rosa's outfit. Her rose-and-yellow patterned swing dress had a row of large white buttons running down the bodice and a white patent leather belt accenting her narrow waist. She finished off the outfit with yellow heels, the ankle straps tied into dainty bows. Rosa had discarded her first ragged satchel bag, a temporary accessory used when the need was urgent, and had accumulated several new cat-carrying bags to replace it.

Her second-floor office was the last door on the left down the wide, carpeted hallway that ran past several law firms and busy accounting businesses. A large window at the end of the hall overlooked the street below. Rosa stepped back to regard the freshly painted lettering on the frosted glass that made up the upper half of the oak door—*Reed Investigations*.

A few days ago, when the sign painters had put the final touches on the lettering, she had snapped a picture of it to send to her parents. She knew they would burst with pride at the sight of her name on the door. Rosa had spent a large part of her youth working with her mother, Ginger Reed, at the office of *Lady Gold Investigations and* credited that time for her apparent aptitude for sleuthing. She'd also learned from her work as a female member of the London Metropolitan Police. As her father, Basil Reed, a superintendent at Scotland Yard, liked to say, the apple didn't fall far from the tree.

Rosa slid the key into the lock, opened the door,

and gently put her satchel down on the blue-padded cushions of the teakwood, Danish-style sofa that served as reception area seating. Diego immediately jumped out to explore the room.

With Gloria's help—her cousin had decided to study interior design, and Rosa couldn't help but wonder how long this particular passion would last—Rosa had outfitted the office to match the Spanish mission design of the building. Brightened by sunlight streaming in from a large window, the room had an impressive view of Santa Bonita's business district. Green- leather-padded chairs circled a Spanish-mission-inspired coffee table. Adjacent to that was a matching desk. A set of shelves lined a portion of one wall, which Rosa planned to fill with books.

She'd already order certain law reference books and other resources such as textbooks on modern forensics and police investigative practices. A few mysteries and detective novels she'd picked up at the local bookstore lined one of the shelves along with a set of history encyclopedias and certain literary works of famous authors like Mark Twain and Ralph Waldo Emerson.

Rosa wanted the office to have a comfortable and inspiring ambiance. A kitchenette at one end of the office featured a small range, refrigerator, and cupboards for dishes and minimal food storage. A cast iron bistro table sat in the corner with two chairs, which suited the Spanish terracotta tiling on the floor.

An adjoining door opened to a darkroom, much

like the one in her mother's office in London. Rosa had purchased an Argus 35 mm camera, like the one she had used for her police work. Not only was she adept at using the camera but also, she did a fine job developing the photographs. It was much faster and easier than taking the film to a photo processing lab.

Diego immediately curled up on a chair, while Rosa removed her sunglasses, scarf, and gloves and set them on a side table. Settling into her desk chair, she arranged her crinoline slip and her skirt then stared out of the window at the vehicles rumbling down the street.

Rosa's gaze settled on the recently installed black telephone, which seemed to mock her with its silence. For a moment, she felt a twinge of doubt. Had she been presumptuous in her decision to stay in California? Who was she to think that her assisting the Santa Bonita Police would cause anyone to seek her out for private investigating? Not only was she not American (her British accent an instant giveaway), but she was also a woman. Two definite strikes against her when it came to competing for work. And then there was Detective Miguel Belmonte—her pulse raced a little at the thought of him.

The thought of returning to London made Rosa's stomach twist. She hadn't recovered from the unsolved murder of her good friend, Lady Vivien Eveleigh, not to mention facing the tabloids who'd had a heyday after she'd abandoned her fiancé, Lord Winston Eveleigh, Vivien's brother, at the altar.

And there was Larry. Rosa and the assistant medical examiner, Dr. Larry Rayburn, had been on several dates since she'd given him her number back in June, and she found his Texas charm delightful.

Besides that, Aunt Louisa had made it clear that the Forrester mansion was Rosa's home for as long as she wanted to stay. While her cousin Clarence had been indifferent, Gloria had been ecstatic. "Maybe I should take up journalism after all. We could work together!"

"Who knows?" Rosa had replied, laughing. Her cousin's mind changed like the wind. "Anything is possible. Let's see what happens."

That seemed Rosa's motto these days. Let's see what happens, let the wind take the sails, or *que sera sera,* as she had recently heard Doris Day sing on the radio.

The shrill ring of the telephone, a sound she hadn't yet heard, startled Rosa. Who could it be? She hadn't even given out her number to anyone. Perhaps someone who'd seen the advertisement she'd placed in *The Santa Bonita Gazette*, but it had only come out this morning. This couldn't already be a client?

"Miss Rosa Reed from Reed Investigations." Rosa smiled to herself as she uttered the words for the first time.

"Hello, Miss Reed." The voice was throaty and

female. "My name is Mrs. Gainer. I hope you can help me."

"I'll do my best, Mrs. Gainer," Rosa replied. "What is it that you need?"

"I have an uncle, well it's through marriage actually, my husband's uncle."

Rosa waited. It was obvious the lady was trying to collect herself.

"He's an odd character, you see. Every family has one of those, don't they?"

Rosa agreed, her mind going to Aunt Louisa and Grandma Sally. "Sometimes, more than one."

"Well, my husband's uncle's name is Dieter Braun. He's been missing for four days, and I think he's in trouble." Mrs. Gainer's voice grew somber. "I think he's been kidnapped or...maybe even worse!"

Buy on AMAZON or read for free with Kindle Unlimited!

ABOUT THE AUTHORS

Lee Strauss is a USA TODAY bestselling author of The Ginger Gold Mysteries series, The Higgins & Hawke Mystery series, The Rosa Reed Mystery series (cozy historical mysteries), A Nursery Rhyme Mystery series (mystery suspense), The Perception series (young adult dystopian), The Light & Love series (sweet romance), The Clockwise Collection (YA time travel romance), and young adult historical fiction with over a million books read. She has titles published in German, Spanish and Korean, and a growing audio library.

Denise Jaden is the author of several contemporary novels for teens and nonfiction books for writers. She splits her time between writing, dancing with a Polynesian dance troupe, and acting with the Vancouver film industry. Find out more about Denise at denisejaden.com.

For more info on books by Lee Strauss and her social media links, visit leestraussbooks.com. To make sure you don't miss the next new release, be sure to sign up for her readers' list!

Did you know you can follow your favorite authors on Bookbub? If you subscribe to Bookbub — (and if you don't, why don't you? - They'll send you daily emails alerting you to sales and new releases on just the kind of books you like to read!) — follow me to make sure you don't miss the next Ginger Gold Mystery!

www.leestraussbooks.com
leestraussbooks@gmail.com

ACKNOWLEDGMENTS

Many thanks to my editors Angelika Offenwanger, Robbi Bryant, and Heather Belleguelle! I couldn't do this without you guys!

My gratitude extends to my co-writer and overall partner in life and crime, Norm Strauss. Not only for helping me jump start this series with plotting, and jotting first drafts, but for joining me on this adventure called life. I *really* couldn't do it without you.

Special thanks to my long-time, in-real-life friend Denise Jaden for her work on the story and for just being an awesome person.

And to Jesus, always faithful.

CPSIA information can be obtained
at www.ICGtesting.com
Printed in the USA
BVHW031723270820
587482BV00001B/129